'A journey   ly)

'Sometime o.., 1994, Kurt
Cobain, the lead singer of Nirvana, killed himself with a
single shot to the head. He wrote a one-page note in red ink,
addressing it to "Boddah", his childhood imaginary friend...'
(Taken from a Cobain web 'shrine')

Welcome to rainy Aberdeen, a small logging town
near Seattle, sometime in the early 1990s. Homer
'Boddah' Alienson is a lonely insomniac who spends
his days selling toys by mail order, and his nights
watching *Twin Peaks* and the first Gulf War unfold on
TV. Homer has always lived a life apart – until the day
he meets a boy named Kurt, loafing about under a
bridge. It is Kurt who reveals to Homer the way to
sleep: heroin, nirvana...

'A powerful, well-written story... forceful and beautiful'
BEN FACCINI, author of *The Water-breather*

Love-Shaped Story

The names, facts and places in this novel do not in any way represent people and events in the real world. Biographical truth does not exist, and even if it did we would not know what to do with it.

Tommaso Pincio

Love-Shaped Story
Translated from the Italian
by Jon Hunt

Flamingo

Flamingo
An imprint of HarperCollins*Publishers*
77–85 Fulham Palace Road,
Hammersmith, London W6 8JB

Flamingo is a registered trade mark of
HarperCollins*Publishers* Limited

www.harpercollins.co.uk

Published by Flamingo 2004
3 5 7 9 8 6 4 2

First published in Italian as
Un amore dell'altro mondo by Einaudi

A catalogue record for this book
is available from the British Library

ISBN 0 00 715401 1

Set in Swift

Printed and bound in Great Britain by
The Bath Press, Bath

To Kurt Cobain

'Now it is well known that when there are many of these flowers together their odor is so powerful that anyone who breathes it falls asleep, and if the sleeper is not carried away from the scent of the flowers, he sleeps on and on forever.'

L. FRANK BAUM, *The Wonderful Wizard of Oz*

1.

Smalltown Alien

What about love?

It was approaching the turn of the last century. The Nineties, as they were then known – the years of creeping unease, as they have since been called – had just begun. Homer B. Alienson, a human being who had already used up more than half his natural life expectancy, stepped out into the new decade with this question ringing in his brain: 'What about love?'

Everyone was haunted by questions back then. Questions like 'Who killed Laura Palmer?' So there was no reason for Homer to be surprised when this unwelcome query started pestering him. It was in the air. Sooner or later, he too was bound to have his life needlessly disrupted, be confronted by a problem that had never before *been* a problem to him.

He was indeed expecting it. But he was hoping to avoid the problem, find some system for being overlooked, missed out, some tiny gap in the registers that charted the flood of living beings. But he was the first to doubt that he could really count on such unlikely eventualities, and even on his brighter days he couldn't imagine himself truly safe. There are some things you just can't avoid; they're bound to happen sooner or later. But at least let it be later, let him be granted a reprieve.

2   It wasn't that he'd never thought about it. It wasn't that he didn't know what love was. He hadn't done anything about it yet, he was prepared to admit that, but what was the hurry, anyway? Why now? Why him? Why didn't they take their questions somewhere else? Why didn't they leave him alone, when with his space toys and his system of life he wasn't bothering anybody? It wasn't that he wanted to avoid the problem; all he asked for was a bit of peace and quiet. He would think about this love thing, he knew he was going to have to do something about it. Just, not now.

They came from far away, such questions. From far, far away – so far away, they were already posing themselves long before you were born. Formulating themselves in some dark primordial pit, they devoured lightless years to come and seek you out in the grayest holes in the universe, in places you wouldn't have wandered into even by mistake − places you'd never have found even if you'd been looking for them.

And was there a grayer hole in the world than Aberdeen? It did nothing but rain there, the constant drizzle echoing the steady fall of chopped-down trees. Not a trace of its colorful past now remained; the 'women's boardinghouses' of Hume Street were a thing of the past. All that was left was a wasteland of lumberyards beside the river Wishkah and the smell of rain-soaked wood. With time, even the loggers had been supplanted by machinery. The wood was cut with lasers now, and there was nothing left to do except go and get drunk in taverns like the Pourhouse, or jump off a bridge.

There were said to be more suicides in Grays Harbor County than anywhere else in the country. And yet people needed that record. It instilled calm, it seemed to explain things that didn't bear explanation. People heard about their highest rate of suicides and it made them feel better. Not exactly good, just better. But this was a place where one of the highlights of the year was the annual chainsaw championships. Not to mention that sky, the cheerless evergray sky of Aberdeen.

Homer could sit musing for hours on that color, and on the real substance of what were perhaps only apparently clouds. Prehistoric clouds that had already been there in the age of the dinosaurs. Clouds too heavy to be scattered or dragged off somewhere else by the wind. He looked at those clouds and it occurred to him that they were the reason why there was no space base in Grays Harbor County. You wouldn't have a hope of getting a rocket into space from there. He imagined the rocket lifting off, then dwindling in size till it vanished at the end of a trail of whitish smoke. Then he heard a boom and saw bits of metal raining from the sky, and he realized they were the fragments of the rocket falling back to earth. Not even rockets could pierce the evergray vault of Aberdeen.

What about love?

He couldn't remember exactly when the question had first appeared, but he had reason to believe that it had been on one of those hopeless noontides when he would slump on the couch and sit there motionless, contemplating the grayness that seeped in through the window. It must have fallen from the sky in a single frozen moment, a rain effect in stop-motion created by fragments of one of those rockets that failed to pierce the vault of Aberdeen.

This kind of inductive memory only served to insinuate the question yet more deeply into his mind. Homer knew very well that he wouldn't break free of it easily. He knew very well that it wouldn't let him alone till he'd given it an answer. And not an evasive answer, either. He would have to present a plan of the steps he intended taking to address the total lack of love in his life, give a precise and credible account of what he meant to do, how he would go about it, and above all, when. In other words he would have to show some initiative – that is to say, venture onto ground that was definitely not his forte.

At the time when the question first appeared, Homer B. Alienson's life was drifting along on a current of placid sadness, like one of the dark logs dragged along by the waters of the Wishkah. The only difference was that whereas the Wishkah had a goal in the ocean, the river of his life flowed monotonously on toward nothing. Or rather, given the manner in which whole days died without the slightest hope of being remembered for anything, the waters of the river Homer followed a course more similar to the cycle of a washing machine.

On the first of every month he went to the Laundromat, stuffed his dirty, malodorous washing into the drum, trying not to touch the metal because it gave him the shivers, elbowed the door shut, put the detergent in the drawer, selected the program, switched on the washing machine, sat down and allowed himself to be melancholically hypnotized by the vortex of the washes and rinses. The movement of his dirty washing took on the features of his thoughts, those thoughts that for a whole month he had not been aware of having and that he could scarcely now recognize as his own. The noise that accompanied the end of the cycle always caught him unprepared and when the drum came to a complete stop, Homer felt a grief take the place of his soul, as if somebody had died, whereupon he clicked open the door with his elbow and stuffed his washing into his bag. The thoughts that a short while earlier he had seemed to descry in the maelstrom of the rinse disappeared, swamped by that familiar, cruel smell of damp, metal and detergent. He zipped up his bag abruptly, as if that gesture in itself were enough to immunize him from the feeling of emptiness into which he knew he must plunge, but there were the plastic chairs and the false ceiling of the Laundromat, and the grayness and the wet streets outside, all just waiting to seize him by the throat. And it was in that frame of mind that he'd go home.

Still, apart from the monthly episodes at the Laundromat, Homer didn't feel things were going all that badly. Not a great deal happened in his life, and that in itself was an advantage, because he wasn't the sort of person who could face up to things, and coming to terms with a new situation cost him a good deal of time and energy. By adopting a particular system for living he had also solved an insomnia problem that he had formerly suffered from. What's more, business was thriving and his mail-order sales of space toys brought in what little he needed to live on. The thought of the number of people who were interested in those objects and the sums they were prepared to pay in order to possess them was sufficient gratification, his childhood's revenge on the laws of the civilized world.

When he was a kid he adored space toys; he was so crazy about them that he cajoled his parents into giving him the same one over and over again. They weren't at all happy about this fixation of his; they were afraid he'd become one of those rather dumb, introverted kids who can't cope with life when they grow to adulthood. So it was with good intentions – though in vain – that they tried to get him to see reason, bring him back to normality.

'What the hell do you want another one for? You've already got five,' they'd say, but he just wouldn't listen. There was no way of getting him to change his mind.

For Christmas 1964 he asked for a flying saucer gun. He already had four, but he wanted a fifth and was determined to get it. His mother refused. She told him she had no intention of continuing with this nonsense. She defended her decision with nebulous arguments about the immoral wastefulness of continuing to spend money on the same toy.

'Immoral?' said Homer, who harbored doubts about the logic of her argument, let alone the meaning of the word immoral.

'Immoral is buying the same thing five times when once is more than enough.'

'You go to the store every day and always buy the same things.'

'That's different.'

'Why's it different?'

'Because the things I buy get used.'

'Flying saucer guns get used too.' His mother's logic was fatally flawed.

'Don't argue. I'm telling you it's different.'

'It isn't different.'

'Yes it is.'

'No it isn't.'

'Yes.'

'No.'

'Listen, I don't care what you say, I'm not buying you another flying saucer gun.'

'Well, I don't care what *you* say, I want another one.'

On Christmas morning Homer came downstairs convinced he had won the argument, but the package under the tree was too shapeless to contain the present he had asked for. He picked it up and gazed at it apprehensively. It was heavy – too heavy for a plastic gun. It had a strange texture and seemed grainy to the touch. He unwrapped it and to his utter dismay found himself looking at a piece of coal. Homer stood there contemplating this affront. His mother had been in a bad mood for the past few days because of some quarrel she'd had with Dad. But what did that have to do with him? He felt himself sinking into the cold grayness that immersed his home and the town of Aberdeen and Grays Harbor County and Washington

State and all the other united states of America and the separated states of the whole world. There rose within him such a rage that he squeezed the piece of coal till it hurt, flung it at a window and ran upstairs to his bedroom, fleeing the sound of shattering glass. He took one of his school notebooks and started tearing out the blank pages one by one. He wrote the same thing on every leaf: 'Message to the people of Aberdeen. Homer B. Alienson hates his Mom because his Mom hates him because his Dad hates her. Everyone hates everyone and I just want to cry.' Then he ran downstairs with the sheets of paper and a roll of adhesive tape, dashed out of the house before his mother could say or do anything and tramped round the neighborhood sticking his proclamation of pain on every door.

A few days later he found the fifth flying saucer gun on his bed. He had gotten what he wanted, but he wasn't exactly satisfied. He almost always did get everything he wanted during that period of his life, because his parents had split up in a manner that, at the age of only seven, had taken away all his joy in living. Gratifying his strange determination to possess dozens of copies of the same toy was the least compensation his parents could give him.

He didn't even unwrap those toys. He merely recorded them in a notebook and put them in cardboard boxes which he sealed with packing tape to keep out the dust and everything else. Why he did this, even he didn't know. Maybe the world frightened him and, not knowing how to defend himself, he was trying at least to defend something that belonged to him. Maybe he was driven by an impulse like that which impelled the pharaohs to have themselves buried along with their treasures. Maybe he saw life as a pyramid, a funerary labyrinth fitted with hidden traps. But if that was the case, he wasn't aware of it. He simply did what he felt like doing, and went on doing it for a long time. Then one day, in that mysterious way that, sooner or later, children stop doing certain things, that obsessive inclination of Homer's sank into oblivion. It re-emerged several years later in a different form, one day when he was in Olympia, the state capital. He had happened to enter one of those stores for collectors that sell old comics and science-fiction books in little plastic bags. He had never been into one of these places, mainly because there weren't any in Aberdeen and he seldom went to Olympia. The place reeked of nostalgia, and Homer felt a shiver run through him, a mixture of cold and sweetness, as if the mangled corpse of a beautiful girl had climbed out of the plastic wrapper in which it was lying to creep up behind him and kiss him on the neck.

A bell tinkled as the door opened. Homer turned and saw the sheets of paper pinned to the noticeboard stir in the gust of cold air that had blown into the store. For no particular reason he started reading the requests and offers. He received a strange impression of the people who'd written them – they seemed to him like unhappy ghosts, tormented souls who sought illusory relief in an unobtainable issue of some comic lost in time, a time only they remembered. He imagined them as zombies, creatures that had suffered terrible mutilations at some point in their lives. People disfigured by fast-food joints and department stores, corroded by irreversible degenerative processes. Overweight guys who lay hidden for most of the time, who gradually lost the capacity for social living, who ventured out onto the streets furtively, sidling along walls, constantly looking over their shoulders, starting at the slightest sign of misunderstood hostility – a pair of eyes met by chance or the distant cry of a mother scolding her child. People whom Homer feared he might one day grow to resemble and in whom he refused to recognize himself.

True, he himself kept relics of his space-age childhood packed away in boxes at home, but that didn't make him a collector. Collectors are usually people who are perversely searching for something they will never be able to possess or have lost forever, something captured, deep-frozen, in the collected object. And the rarer the object, the deeper-frozen is the anxiety of the search. But Homer wasn't searching for anything. He had stored away his space toys in real time, on the spot, when he was still a kid, when they were among the easiest things to find. In a sense he had stored away provisions in the same way as ants or people in fall-out shelters do. And now he was like an ant that had been told that the planet was heading for global desertification and that in a few years' time there would be no more winters, even in the Antarctic. He was like an ordinary man who had invested his savings in an underground bunker dug in his backyard only to learn that the Cold War was going to end, with worldwide nuclear disarmament. He had accumulated enough robots and spaceships to immunize himself for all eternity against any form of nostalgia. He no longer felt any affection for those toys, sealed up in their packets. Quite the reverse, in fact – at the memory of his sufferings as a child, he loathed them.

To him they were indissolubly linked to his unequal struggle for survival in a world of adults who could never be trusted. Sometimes he had felt an urge to take the boxes and throw them all into the river off the North Aberdeen Bridge in the hope of breaking the circle of nothingness that imprisoned him. The only thing that stopped him doing so was a superstitious respect for those guiltless toys. He reflected that, after all, they were the only living part of the child he had once been and that for this reason alone they deserved to be saved.

When he read the ad in the store in Olympia, Homer sensed an opportunity. 'DESPERATELY seeking Yonezawa Moon Explorer. Up to $150 offered for specimen in good condition. Jim (206) 352-ITEM', it said. The accompanying photograph was hopelessly blurred, but Homer didn't need its help. He was well acquainted with the Yonezawa Moon Explorer, and if he remembered correctly there must be at least two under his bed, their packaging still intact. The toy was a Japanese-made lunar exploration module about eight inches long. A tin-and-plastic gadget with an amazing range of functions that could be remote-controlled from a handset shaped like a rocket. Rotating aerial, flashing lights, lunar module sound effects, openable central hatch.

But it wasn't a particularly attractive object to look at. It was made of shoddy materials and to a rather rough-and-ready design which made it unconvincing. The usual cheap 1950s Japanese product that wasn't worth buying more than twice. It was undoubtedly one of the more expendable objects in his store.

All things considered, why not? This guy seemed really keen on the Yonezawa Moon Explorer, to judge from the way he'd written DESPERATELY. The toys Homer had persuaded his parents to buy him when he was a kid were doomed to remain mummified in their packages, and there was no denying that a hundred and fifty dollars was a tidy sum. He tore off one of the strips of paper bearing Jim's phone number and as soon as he got home called him.

352-ITEM.

It was a difficult conversation, stifled by pauses and awkwardness. At the sound of the mumbling, breathless voice at the other end of the line, Homer felt a sense of unbearable anguish. Eventually he made a deal with the guy, but when he hung up he felt sad and drained. He went out for a walk. The sky was so oppressive that his state of mind worsened.

Jim had asked him if he happened to have any other spacecraft to sell. Homer's reply was deliberately vague. If he'd given him an inkling of what he had at home, Jim would never have stopped pestering him till the end of his days. He said maybe he did, he'd check.

'Great,' enthused Jim. 'A-and can I call you tomorrow? To find out?'

'No,' Homer replied bluntly, and followed this up with a barefaced lie: 'I'm not on the phone. If I find anything I'll write and tell you when I send you the Moon Explorer.'

What does this retard take me for? thought Homer. Some sort of nostalgia geek, like him? Jesus, I'm a normal person. Let's just keep our distance, here, shall we?

So that's what he did. He kept his distance. He told Jim he'd let him know where to send the check, then went to the post office, got a mailbox and called him back.

'P.O. Box 911. Aberdeen.'

'P-pack it carefully, please,' Jim implored him.

'It's been packed away carefully for years,' said Homer curtly.

'Oh,' said Jim, not quite knowing how to take this. 'A-and about the possibility of other...'

'I'll let you know.'

'Y-yes, but don't forget.'

'Don't worry, I won't.' He hung up and thought, Jesus, am I right to keep my distance from these guys.

Then he went out to take another walk in the woods before the rain came.

By the time the question of love appeared to disrupt the placid insignificance of Homer's days, his mail-order sales of space toys had burgeoned into a regular business. Of course, they weren't going to make him rich, but his needs were pretty basic. Apart from the special system he needed to make him sleep.

His first contact with Jim was followed by others. Numerous similar geeks, who'd gotten his address from Jim, started sending desperate appeals to Homer's mailbox at the rate of a dozen per week. They asked him for rarities like the Yoshiya Space Scout 7, the Horikawa satellite target practice kit, the Nomura Planet-Y space station, the mobile TV unit, also made by Nomura, the legendary Rex Mars battle rocket, and the atomic water pistol with a red handle shaped like a light bulb, a pistol 'guaranteed to atomize any space invader'. All articles of which Homer had at least two copies in stock and for which his customers' offers ranged from a hundred to a hundred and fifty dollars.

He only needed to sell a couple per week to make a decent living, and, at a conservative estimate, if he maintained that average his stock of space toys would last for another seven years. He thought about this. Seven years was a long time; a lot can happen in seven years. But he didn't make a systematic plan. He decided to consider each case on its merits, toy by toy, request by request. Maybe he could try gradually raising the prices, or holding impromptu auctions to eke out his stocks. Two hundred dollars per item would be enough to keep him going for fourteen years. And what was two hundred dollars for one of his perfectly preserved rarities?

He felt that he could risk it; those guys would go to any lengths to get their clammy hands on one of his toys. Well, maybe not all of them. But some, for sure. The most regressive of them would probably kill to get hold of one, let alone spend a measly two hundred dollars. Maybe even three hundred. Which would mean, to Homer, survival for another seven years. Twenty-one years in all, not bad. Twenty-one years doing fuck all. Just selling toys. Just reading the requests and deciding which of them to grant. Waiting for the check and taking the package containing the sold toy to the post office.

He decided to quit his job as night janitor at the Aberdeen Public Library. It wasn't bad, the library job. It was something to do, and it was one more reason for staying awake at night, though he had so many reasons that half as many would have been enough. Also, it was a safe place; somewhat funereal perhaps, but safe. And then he liked the way the echo of his footsteps in the reading room seemed to call forth the rain that arrived unfailingly every night. The gentle patter of the rain and the echo of his footsteps in the reading room. There was a kind of beauty in that.

But what would he do if the opportunity of closing his eyes should present itself, as eventually it did? To go on keeping a night watch over the Public Library's books would have been to set a professional seal on his sleepless condition. Quitting that job was essential if he was to keep his hopes up and be ready for the great moment when he would be able to lie down on his bed without having to fit his eyes with the *Clockwork Orange*-style anti-sleep clips he'd made for himself, without getting pins and needles in his arms from holding phials of eye drops over his eyes.

He had a hunch that some day or other he would find a sure system, so he decided to quit the library job. It would really suck if, when he finally found the system, he had to stay awake anyway for professional reasons. For it was only a matter of time. Sooner or later he, too, would savor the sweet fade of drowsiness, the soft abyss of sleep approaching, the warmth of the house receding toward the sharp wetness of the woods. He would savor these things, no longer forced to tap his steps to the muffled murmur of the rain. Nights with nothing in them anymore. Just nights. At last.

Homer B. Alienson quit sleeping a couple of years after the incident involving the piece of coal, at age nine. He was still a kid, but had seen and suffered enough to understand that the adult world on which he was forced to depend was not to be trusted. He'd discovered that the places where you feel protected are the very ones that conceal the most insidious threats, and he'd realized that the happiness of his childhood years was only apparent. It had all been leading up to the time when he would fall into a trapdoor of misery that he would climb back out of with his heart's bones broken.

He quit sleeping because he'd noticed something suspicious about people, starting with his closest relatives.

Starting with his mother, to take the most terrible example. He didn't know why, but he was sure that she and all the others were out to get him. It wasn't so much the manifestations of open hostility – like the coal Christmas present – that put him on the alert, but a sinister, indefinable essence. There was something wrong about people; they didn't seem to be what they *should* have been. They hadn't changed much since he had first begun to become aware of their existence. And yet, starting on a day that Homer couldn't place precisely in the past, a day that wandered around in his memories like a child that's lost its parents, they had seemed different. They hadn't changed, yet they were different. If he'd been asked to explain what the difference consisted of, he would have been hard put to it. The difference that he had in mind was indefinable, baseless. It was difference *per se*. Difference in the most different sense of the word. It was the classic example of a situation that can only be explained in the absolute, what Homer called an absolute spectrum situation.

Besides, it wasn't as if he could go and explain to anyone. Who could he explain *to*? There was nobody left. Everybody was different, from his mother to the garbage man. What was he supposed to do? Go up to his mother and say, 'Mom, why are you so different?'

'Different?' she'd reply. 'What on earth are you talking about, Home?' That was what she called him, Home.

'You seem different to me, Mom.'

'*How* am I different?'

'You seem like. . .' He'd have to be careful how he put this. One false step and he'd give himself away.

'Yes, Home?'

'Like the garbage man,' he'd say, at length. Which certainly wouldn't be one of the smartest things to say. But he wouldn't be able to stop himself, he'd blurt it out. And give himself away. Thereby ruining any chance he had of maintaining the status quo, of continuing to live without having to confront the difference that was spreading all around him.

The maintenance of the status quo was vital. What would happen to him when the others found out that he wasn't different as they were? Then, one day, he understood. The difference was revealed to him in all its essence. He understood that, quite simply, his mother *was not* his mother and the garbage man *was not* the garbage man. Nobody was who they were, except him. Only he had remained the Homer he was.

It was the TV that revealed this to him. In 1967, toward the end of February, Homer B. Alienson saw documented on the small screen a situation alarmingly similar to the one in which he found himself. A little boy called Jimmy Grimaldi was dragged along by his grandmother to the office of one Dr Miles Bennell. The kid seemed to be having hysterics; he kept screaming that his mother wasn't his mother and pleading with them not to take him home, or she'd get him. Dr Bennell, who for obvious filmic reasons had the fine features of a refined, well-mannered movie actor, prescribed some pills to be taken a certain number of times a day and advised the grandmother to keep the boy at her house for a while. Then, with a thoughtful look on his face, the doctor decided to pay a visit to Wilma Lentz, the cousin of an old flame of his, one Becky Driscoll, whose gentle charm found its own conventional personification in the beautiful Dana Wynter, a movie actress who bore a faint resemblance to Elizabeth Taylor.

Wilma, a woman in her thirties, is in a similar state to little Jimmy Grimaldi: she's convinced her Uncle Ira is not her Uncle Ira.

The doctor watches the tranquil old man pushing the lawnmower up and down the lawn and doesn't know what to think. The similarity to the case of the little boy is undoubtedly curious. But Miles Bennell is a man of science and as such can only draw one conclusion.

'Obviously the boy's mother was his mother, I'd seen her. And Uncle Ira was Uncle Ira, there was no doubt of that after I'd talked to him,' he said off-screen, after advising Wilma to see a 'doctor' friend of his. This, he made quite clear, meant seeking psychiatric help.

If Homer confided in his mother, or in anybody else, as Jimmy and Wilma had done, the same would probably happen to him. They'd make him see a shrink. And although he didn't know exactly what went on in such people's offices, he had a pretty good idea that it wouldn't be pleasant.

That piece of film showed him that 'difference' was not confined to the dreary township in the bleak Northwest where he'd had the misfortune to be born. The same kind of difference that Homer had observed in Aberdeen was present in all its disturbing virulence elsewhere in the world too. Such a universal and constantly spreading phenomenon certainly couldn't be stopped by a nine-year-old boy.

It was impossible for him to get away. All he could do was devise techniques of passive defense, try not to do anything that might jeopardize the status quo, try to blend in with the 'differents' around him. Here the film evidence was a great help, for the director had not merely revealed to the world the invasion of the differents – conventionally described as 'body snatchers', a term that conveyed very well the appalling nature of the change that was taking place – but had also given two crucial pieces of practical advice. First: what you had to do to avoid being body-snatched – integrated into the change that was taking place. Second: how you could conceal your extraneousness to the replicants – your intention not to be changed.

As far as the second point was concerned, no great effort was required. You simply had to feign indifference to the differents' hostility. Be impermeable. Not let them rile you. The differents always acted in a deliberately hostile manner, to provoke normal people into giving themselves away. Homer's violent reaction to the provocation of the Christmas piece of coal, for instance, was something to be avoided. He had probably only gotten away with it because he was a kid. But who was to know how long the period of immunity would last, and when the time of integration would begin? He decided he'd better be careful, and immediately adopted the recommended behavior. Impermeability. Insensibility. He resolved to reduce communication with others to a minimum, and spent all the time on his own, concentrating on his collection of space toys.

But if the second point wasn't much of a problem,

the first – how to avoid being body-snatched – had a drastic solution. It was perfectly simple in theory, but in practice . . . in practice it meant giving up sleeping. Because that was how the change came about. You fell asleep and you woke up different.

In the film footage, Dr Bennell had spoken of how people often became dehumanized, losing their identity so gradually that they weren't aware of any alteration in themselves.

Homer couldn't agree more. That was exactly how it had happened. His mother, the garbage man and all the others. The change was imperceptibly slow until the final, irrevocable moment of palpable difference. But this didn't make it any easier to accept the drawbacks of the solution. It's all very well to talk, but how are you supposed to react when somebody comes along and tells you it's quite easy, all you have to do is not sleep?

All you have to do, he says.

Homer Alienson's voluntary insomnia continued for an extraordinary length of time. Nigh on eighteen years, give or take a month or two. This was not an easy period, nor was it devoid of consequences. It was an established scientific fact, even in those days, that the

solidity of objects and the menacing hostility of the human race. If ever he had been destined to experience moments of happiness, those moments must have been the early days of the system. They were his golden age, his paradise lost, his nirvana before death.

Unfortunately, the era of happiness in which he thought he was living receded, slowly but remorselessly, into the past. Eventually it vanished completely, except for occasional flashes, sadistic manifestations that only served to intensify his regret, to heighten his oppressive nostalgia for those halcyon days. Reluctantly, Homer was forced to conclude that one of the strengths of the system was precisely this: the elusiveness of its beginnings. And that was what made it so desperately desirable; so intimately indispensable.

He realized, in other words, that his unconditional subjection was explained by his anxiety to rediscover that indescribable glow that he thought he'd glimpsed in the early times. *Beginning to see the light*, he'd heard someone sing once on the radio. That was exactly how he had felt. He had begun to see the light – a light connected, in his memory, with the dawn glow of that day when he had returned home with the little pouch of system in the right pocket of his sweatpants. Then everything had gone blank.

With the passing of time he discovered that the more use he made of the system, the more his need to relive the feelings of the early days increased, while still remaining unsatisfied; the more he systemized his life, the weaker the feelings he was seeking became. He began to form the conviction that the whole complex of his sensory capacities had undergone a radical and irreversible change. He began to suspect that he no longer experienced things in the same way; that he no longer had feelings – at least not in the sense that he thought he should attribute to the concept of feeling. If he'd been obliged to explain the phenomenon, he would probably have said that feelings had been replaced by states, ranging from the transitory state of wellbeing he'd felt in the early days to a perpetual state of discomfort (the prevailing state from a certain moment onward), with, in between, a wide range of other states, all of them tending toward the negative.

After a while he understood that the fundamental state, the one that determined the nuances and gradations of all the others, was his addiction to the system. It occurred to him that it might be a good idea to change his system of life. And he tried to do so, at least initially. He tried to give up the system and return to the heroic Spartan sleeplessness of the presystemic age. He discovered, however, that it wasn't so easy to escape; he felt the overwhelming strength of the system and discovered how much he had come to depend on it; he discovered that the perpetual state of discomfort was nothing compared to the pain that awaited him beyond the protective cushion; he discovered that if you live even for a short time in a world of foam rubber, contact with the hard material of things and the rough minds of people hurts too much; he discovered that when you return to feelings after living in states, the only feeling open to you is that of pain; he discovered pain in all its forms, a species of pain unknown to those who had never entered the system; he came to know pain as a form of life and discovered that pain itself could become a system, a far more invasive and unbearable system than the one that enabled him to sleep. For this and other reasons he never really tried to leave the system. Never even contemplated it. When you're inside it, the thought of leaving is only a dream, a way of deluding yourself and killing time. And when, in the early Nineties, the question of love was put to him, he couldn't remember ever having had a thought that had even the remotest connection with the possibility of leaving it.

The system had gradually and definitively gained the upper hand, so that now it was no longer appropriate to speak of Homer being totally systemized, but rather of the system being homerized. Totally.

The day when the dawn light had been the color of steel and he'd returned home to gaze at his thoughts mirrored in the little bag of system that Kurt had given him, was a day of eager expectation. After cracking his knuckles and sighing, Homer had made up his mind not to try the system until the evening. He wanted to perform the act with due ceremony. It must have all the solemnity of an official occasion, so he would have to devise an appropriate ritual. He had wandered aimlessly round the house, cracking his knuckles at regular intervals, trying to think what might be suitable, but hadn't been able to think of anything except that he found this new trick of cracking his knuckles really rather agreeable. Then he had gone out and walked toward the bus station without any precise intention. He lined up for tickets, though he had no destination in mind. Only when he found himself at the counter did he return to his senses and realize that he had come all this way for nothing. But he couldn't tell the ticket clerk that he'd made a mistake. He knew himself only too well and was aware that whatever excuse he might have mumbled out would have sounded suspicious to the ticket clerk, who bore all the hallmarks of the classic different. He couldn't risk being caught out after years of sleeplessness and only one step away from the system, so he bought a ticket to Olympia, doing his best to seem decisive. During the journey, with his head resting against the icy glass of the window, not really knowing what he was going to do when he got there, he thought about the beauty of being able to close your eyes and go to sleep, gently rocked by the movement of the bus as it devoured miles of wet asphalt. He peered out of the corner of his eye at the little boy sleeping in the row in front, till the mother noticed and glared back at him. Homer responded with an indignant leer. He meant to communicate to that woman and to the whole company of differents his profound sense of triumph. No longer will you hold me in the palm of your hand, that leer meant. Her only response was to take the child in her arms and move nearer the front, to the seat behind the driver. In the old days such behavior would have made him feel trapped, but now everything was different. He felt secure, and rested his head on the window again, enjoying the vibrations of the icy glass pane. The sight of the sleeping child had reminded him of the evening many years ago when he'd seen the famous piece of film footage that had changed his life. He had never again had occasion to see that recording of the dramatic testimony of Dr Miles Bennell of Santa Mira. The pictures had imprinted themselves on his memory, and every time he thought about them he seemed to relive distinctly the feelings he'd had, but if he tried to reconstruct the events narrated in the film he realized that only scattered fragments remained. He could only recall isolated scenes, like that of the central square of Santa Mira in the morning viewed from Dr Bennell's window, or the one where Dr Bennell crosses the road arm in arm with his old flame Becky Driscoll, or again – more indelible than all the others – the close-up of the wonderful face of Dana Wynter who, toward the end of the film excerpt, personifies the different Becky Driscoll, the one who has turned cold after yielding to the need to sleep. But he couldn't visualize the whole. He wished he could see that footage again, now that he was capable of viewing it from a completely different perspective. He wondered whether it was worth phoning some TV station to ask them to show the footage of the body snatchers. They might listen to him. Maybe they did take notice of what viewers said. Maybe they even had a special slot, called 'Film requests'. He lifted his head off the window and thought the idea was really stupid. He cracked his knuckles and sighed. Then he had a flash of inspiration. Why bother to ask the TV people? What was to stop him doing it all on his own? At once he realized that he had not taken the bus to Olympia in vain and knew what he was going to do as soon as he reached town. First he would go around the stores where they rented videos, looking for film of the body snatchers, then he would buy a VCR. That's what he'd do when he got to town. He was excited, too, at the idea of what he would do when he got home. First he would install the VCR, following all the enclosed instructions, then he would prepare the powdered system, scrupulously following the instructions Kurt had given him, then he would at last try the effects of the system while watching the film of the body snatchers. Fuck it, that was what he'd do. He'd go to sleep watching the film that hadn't let him sleep for eighteen years. Yeah, that was it. To hell with everyone. God is gay, Nixon killed Hendrix and I crack my knuckles, he said to himself, slouching down in his seat.

* * *

He arrived home late in the evening. He'd stopped to eat in one of the fast-food joints on the state highway, just outside town, and had walked the rest of the way. He usually steered clear of those places, but that evening dinner was the last thing on his mind, a physiological chore that separated him from that first, great night with the system.

To facilitate taking the system powder, Kurt had suggested he obtain a straw, and Homer, to be on the safe side, had taken four from the dispenser at the cash desk. On leaving the diner, he'd thanked the dark, cloud-laden heavens for allowing him to be born in a country that had reduced to a minimum the time you had to spend on procuring and consuming food.

Going indoors, he went and sat down on the couch without taking his jacket off. He placed the box containing the VCR on the coffee table and studied the instructions, trying to remember the advice the store assistant had given him – though with scant success, because all the time the man was talking he had been thinking about what it would be like to try the system while he watched, after eighteen years, the film of the body snatchers.

Then he set to work, with some trepidation, because he didn't know much about electrical appliances. But the installation proved less problematic than he expected and, although the timer wouldn't stop blinking 00:00 from the stop position, the machine seemed ready to perform its essential function, the only one that interested Homer at this moment: that of reading the magnetic content of the videocassette so as to decode it into luminous signals that one enjoyed by keeping one's eyes fixed on the TV screen.

Preparing everything necessary for the taking of the system was even easier, because actually there wasn't much to prepare. Kurt had told him to take out of the pouch a large enough dose to systemize himself, which needn't be very much the first time. In fact he had recommended that it be extremely small, though he hadn't seen fit to supply a parameter on the basis of which the quantity might be precisely calculated.

Using the corner of his laminated Aberdeen Public Library card as a measure, Homer extracted this blessed, tiny dose from the little pouch and put it on the Formica top of the coffee table. Kurt had counseled the use of a smooth surface, such as a hand mirror, but since Homer didn't have any hand mirrors in the house, he thought the Formica table top would make a fair substitute, for the time being. On subsequent occasions, if it was really necessary, he would buy a mirror.

Still using the laminated library card, he shaped the extremely small dose of powdered system into a strip about a millimeter thick and just under a half-inch long. Then he took one of the straws into the kitchen and cut it in half. He sat down on the couch again, laying the length of straw next to the strip of powdered system, on the coffee table.

Everything seemed ready. Everything was laid out in accordance with Kurt's instructions. All that remained, apparently, was to take it. The great moment had arrived. The cassette about the body snatchers was inserted the right way round in the VCR. The television was tuned to the VCR channel. All he had to do was press the Play key on the remote control. The opening credits would start to roll and he would take the powdered system through the nose, as Kurt had demonstrated.

He pressed Play.

Your first systemization is rather like your first kiss. You're so preoccupied with the problem of where to put your nose that by the time you realize that that thing you felt on your tongue was actually her tongue, she's already broken away from you.

During the first systemization your dominant thoughts are, first, how long it's going to take for the powder to take effect; second, how you'll know when it *does* take effect; and third, how you can be sure, if at some stage you think it has taken effect, that the feelings you're having are the right ones.

On subsequent occasions, the difference between the system and kisses is that when you kiss you don't think very much about it, whereas when you systemize yourself, whether it's the second or the thousandth time, you do nothing *but* think. You're almost always thinking. Thinking about things like whether this time will be better than the last, because last time wasn't that great, though perhaps that was because maybe you'd had too much to eat, or hadn't had enough to eat, or because it was better to take three small doses at a distance of, say, half an hour from each other, because when you take it all at once the system must be of prime quality, because if there's anything wrong with the system – an eventuality known to people inside the system as 'over-cut' or 'badly cut' or 'shit' – you may, if you shoot too large a quantity, throw up, and then you've wasted system, time and money, not to mention the fact that if the system is too pure even worse can happen.

Such speculation is known to habitués of the system as 'paranoia'. Of course, people outside the system get paranoid, too. But it's not the same thing. Let's take the example of a perfectly ordinary case of paranoid behavior, like leaving home much earlier than necessary because you're convinced that the bus driver, not finding any traffic, will get to the bus stop, say, ten minutes earlier than the regulation time and that, since he is traveling with an empty vehicle and knows perfectly well that at the bus stop in question there's only ever one person waiting, namely you, the person with the delusion of which we are positing an example, he will drive straight past without waiting for the regulation time, and all because you, the paranoiac, have come to the entirely baseless conclusion that the bus driver doesn't like you.

Now, such a delusion would never even enter the head of a true systemizee. But if by some absurd hypothesis it did, he would soon put the matter in perspective. 'What do I care when the fucking bus goes by?' he would say. Note that he would utter these words without the slightest trace of acrimony, and would then continue: 'Look, I may not even go to the bus stop if I don't feel like it. Let him drive past when the fuck he wants. I'm going to stay at home and systemize myself. Who needs buses anyway? I'm never going to take another one for the rest of my life. I'm fine the way I am. I've got the system.'

Nothing in the world is truly important to a person who's inside the system. Everything can be attenuated, viewed in a more reassuring light. No matter how big the problem, it can always be cut down to size. When you're inside the system, having a paranoid delusion that's extraneous to it seems completely meaningless, because the only, essential, constant source of paranoia is your concern with achieving the highest possible degree of integration. All other things are trivial. Decorative problems, ornamental anxieties, non-essential torments. The only thing that matters is integration into the system.

Homer's first time. There's not much to tell, as a matter of fact. What happened was this: as the TV screen framed a sinister sky of shifting white clouds, to the apocalyptic strains of woodwind, strings and rolling drums, Homer bent forward over the coffee table, brought the length of straw to his nose and inhaled the powdered system. At first he felt nothing, except, after a few seconds, a bitter taste in his mouth. He lay back on the couch, convinced he would soon fall asleep. The film continued and when Becky Driscoll, played by the delightful Dana Wynter, made her entry into Miles Bennell's office, Homer was more wide awake than ever. He was still wide awake when it came to the scene where Uncle-Ira-who-isn't-Uncle-Ira pushes the lawnmower across the lawn, exactly as Uncle Ira would do. And he was still wide awake when Becky and Dr Bennell, hunted by the Santa Mira police, who are now themselves in thrall to the difference of the body snatchers, hide in the office and swallow pills to stay awake. This is the scene where it becomes clear once and for all that it's when people are asleep that the body snatchers take their places. So, Becky and Dr Bennell prepare to spend the night in the office and Bennell tells Becky she mustn't close her eyes.

'Or we may wake up changed? To something evil and inhuman?' Becky asks.

'In my practice I've seen how people have allowed their humanity to drain away. Only it happened slowly, instead of all at once. They didn't seem to mind,' muses Bennell.

'Just some people, Miles,' Becky objects.

'All of us, a little bit. We harden our hearts, grow

callous. Only when we have to fight to stay human do we realize how precious it is to us, how dear.'

At this point Miles breaks off, gazes into Becky's dark, fawnlike eyes, her perfect profile silhouetted against the white of the curtain that filters the sinister light from the street, and adds: 'As you are to me.' And as the violins soar, their faces draw together till their lips touch and they kiss.

And it was no good.

He was still awake.

Perfectly, totally, utterly awake.

He should have been getting worried, seeing that a fair time had passed since the beginning of the film footage and his taking of the powder, yet he felt inexplicably calm. He sat there watching those two magnificent specimens of the human race kissing – a sight that would normally have made him very uneasy – as if it were the most natural thing in the world, as if he weren't really there, in front of the TV, as if he were watching from the VIP box of a grand theater full of gilded stuccoes and velvet hangings. Dresses rustled, trails of cigar smoke rose, chandeliers glittered, and a confused murmur of voices mingled with the rustle of the dresses, which took on the smell of the bodies, which rose with the cigar smoke till it reached him in the box where he sat, as he kept his eyes fixed on one sparkling light in particular, a white light that spread outward till it occupied his entire field of vision, till it entered him, entered his body, heating him and relaxing him, a hot, white light that softened his legs and his abdomen, that set his chest ablaze and made first his shoulders then his arms go limp. He was perfect. He was relaxed. He was suspended. He was white. He was everything. He was safe. And he understood. He *understood* . . . Now he understood that he had spent his whole life worrying and protecting himself for nothing. He understood that he had wasted his best years shielding himself from people, from the world, from the differents. He understood that there was nothing to worry about after all. What could they do to him? Who could *ever* have done anything to him? Why had he been so worried? Why had he been so tense? The anxieties of a whole life suddenly seemed incomprehensible.

He watched the film of the body snatchers continue to run, but those alarming pictures that had once revealed the true nature of things to him – those pictures that had been the cause of his not sleeping for eighteen years – didn't disturb him as he'd imagined they would. He was well aware of the dreadful reality depicted in the film, yet it seemed as if all those things didn't concern him, or concerned him only to a certain extent, that they couldn't do him any harm.

Not anymore, anyway.

Not now.

He wondered how this could have happened and whence came this sense of calm that he had never felt in his life before, this white light that heated him from within, this white light of white heat.

He wondered when the system would begin to take effect.

The system that enabled Homer B. Alienson to sleep again – the system that he privately called 'Kurt's system', after the person who introduced him to it – is extracted from the pods of a plant whose scientific name is *Papaver somniferum*, which means the sleep-inducing poppy.

Commonly known as the opium poppy, it is a flower of extraordinary beauty. A black heart encircled by scarlet petals, bobbing at the top of a long stalk, with pods full of gold-green seeds.

It has a long history, stretching back to the lost civilizations of Persia, Egypt and Mesopotamia.

The discovery of some fossilized poppy seeds suggests, indeed, that even Neanderthal man knew how to extract a system of life from this flower so beloved of the Impressionist painters.

He woke up at three in the afternoon. The television was still on and tuned to the VCR channel. Homer couldn't believe he had slept so late. In fact he couldn't even remember sleeping. Nobody really remembers sleeping – even he knew that, despite his scant experience of that state. But he hadn't expected such total darkness.

The last time he'd looked at the clock it had been just before six. The body-snatchers tape had just finished rewinding and Homer had been on the point of starting it again. He'd already seen it twice, and still hadn't fallen asleep. Deciding that he'd been too cautious, he'd inhaled another two lines of powdered system.

There had been high points and low points. Moments of white light with white heat and moments when he wondered when the system was going to take effect. He distinctly remembered seeing for the third time the sinister sky of shifting clouds and hearing the apocalyptic music. He thought he also remembered the scene of Uncle Ira pushing the lawnmower, but couldn't swear to it.

Then he had woken up. Three o'clock in the afternoon. Nine hours. He had slept nine hours and he couldn't believe it. Never before had he erased such a large portion of time from his mind. He knew that this was what happened when you slept, but he wasn't used to it. Such intervals of unconsciousness were a new experience to him.

He had lived the last eighteen years in their entirety, second by second, always conscious of himself and of time. Not that he remembered those years clearly. Far from it. Had he been required to think back through them, it would have taken him no more than a few hours; a day at the very most. But that was because his life had been reduced to a few essential coordinates, a perfect geometry of tedium from which he had never escaped.

There had been times when his thoughts had wandered, it's true. And other times when he'd daydreamed. But he was sure that – if he'd really had to – he could have reconstructed nearly the entire film of those eighteen years, perhaps with the help of some newly invented mind machine or some special memory-enhancing technique.

He straightened up and sat there on the couch, staring at the length of straw and the few grains of system left on the coffee table. The television was emitting its pale blue light and a constant, low electronic hum, but Homer didn't notice. He was in a daze. The signals sent out by the world of physical things were too weak for his present state. He gazed at the coffee table without really seeing anything. His mind, too, was focused on nothing, sweetly void of thought.

All at once, for some inexplicable reason, without anything recalling him to reality, he came to. He emerged from the daze as suddenly as he had fallen into it. At first this puzzled him, especially as he wasn't sure how long that strange, trancelike state had lasted. It couldn't have been more than about ten seconds, but they had been seconds that didn't correspond to one's normal perception of time. Seconds that had slowed down till they almost stopped. Seconds drawn out to their maximum temporal extent, like an elastic band stretched to its limit. Time that had stopped while continuing to flow.

It must be an after-effect of the system, Homer told himself. And if he was really honest, he hadn't found that trancelike state at all disagreeable. He cracked his knuckles and decided to go and stretch his legs in the woods, to breathe the cold, rain-scented air.

He walked for hours, his head full of thoughts that floated away freely, as if they had a life of their own. By the time he got home it was already dark and his thoughts had calmed. They seemed to have become at least partly his own again. He passed by the North Aberdeen Bridge and stopped to talk to Kurt. He wanted to tell him he'd tried the system and to thank him.

He was bursting to talk, which was another new experience for him. He'd never been much of a conversationalist; he was often at a loss for words, and sometimes for subjects too. But on this occasion he spoke fluently, describing in meticulous detail what had happened and what he thought about it.

Kurt listened in silence, nodding as if he already knew that Homer would say all this. He didn't reply until Homer had already bid him goodbye and was walking away, when he called after him:

'Boddah?'

Homer turned. 'Yeah?'

'Go easy with that stuff.'

Homer walked on, wondering what Kurt had meant. As soon as he got home, he went over to the couch and slumped down on it. He hadn't eaten all day, and the TV had been on since he had gone out. But he didn't notice his hunger or the TV.

Question: how did the system reach Aberdeen?

Answer: by a long, circuitous route. The earliest written evidence of man's infatuation with the system dates back to the invention of writing itself, when the Sumerians divulged the secret of the system to the neighboring Akkadians, the latter handed it on to the Assyrians, and the Assyrians, through their trade contacts with the Egyptians and the Syrians, extended the system both westward and northward, taking it even as far as Greece.

Then, thanks to the mercantile enterprise of the Arabs, the system reached China, where with enlightened instruction from the Portuguese the population achieved a degree of integration into the system more total than any previously attained in history. The Portuguese taught the Chinese that there was a method of integration far more powerful than their own one of mixing opium with bamboo juice and boiling it with oatmeal. The new technique, inhaling the system through a pipe, proved highly popular in China, and soon opium dens were opening all over the country.

The Europeans discovered that the system was highly profitable, because it could be used as a cheap exchange commodity for silks, spices, and other exotic articles which the Chinese usually sold at high prices. Consequently the Portuguese were followed in rotation, first by the Dutch, then by the French, and lastly by the British. All of these countries traded with the Chinese, offering their opium system in exchange for precious goods.

The British may have been the last to arrive on the scene, but they were the shrewdest operators of all. They gave an entirely new impetus to the lucrative trade by founding the East India Company, thus laying the basis for addiction to the system on a massive scale. By 1840, there were about three million Chinese doing nothing all day but systemizing themselves in opium dens.

Although the three million Chinese derived great benefits from the system, and regarded it as an indispensable part of their lives, the Chinese government for some reason frowned on this development and decided to ban the system in all its forms. This did not go down well with the British, who risked losing a rich source of income. The result was friction, which on two occasions flared up into open conflicts, referred to in the history books as the First Opium War and the Second Opium War.

While quarrels and battles raged in that part of the world, a considerable number of Chinese – some seventy thousand all told – sailed across the ocean and disembarked in the United States, where they worked on the railroads and in the West-coast gold mines. Some of them, naturally enough, took their pipes with them and began to proselytize among the whites, opening opium dens like those shown in some well-known film footage of the story of Wild Bill Hickock and Calamity Jane, starring Jeff Bridges and Ellen Barkin.

Today many people still imagine that when the gunfighters and cowboys of the Old West came into town, parched with thirst after riding for days across prairies and deserts, the first thing they did was to head for the inevitable saloon – complete with pianist and cancan-dancing hookers – to down a couple of whiskies, usually after limbering up with a hearty fistfight. In actual fact many of them preferred the exotic peace of the opium dens, where they could drift off into dreams of the system, with an attentive young Chinese girl by their side to keep their pipes primed with opium. That's how it all started. That's how the system reached our country.

Question: Okay, that's clear enough as far as it goes. But what about Aberdeen?

Answer: Well, to be honest, the system never actually got that far. Aberdeen was off the circuit, so to speak, and any inhabitant of the town who became dependent on the system was in deep trouble. But Kurt got to know Grunt, a disreputable character with one redeeming feature: he could get you any kind of system you wanted, because he went around robbing pharmacies with his sidekick.

It was Grunt who initiated Kurt into the great world of the system. Kurt was a perfect candidate for addiction: he was sick, he was neurotic, he was a mass of tics, he hated people, and he harbored grudges by the wagonload. He himself was convinced he'd end up as a teenage schizophrenic, the kind of guy that turns up at school one day with an assault rifle and wipes out half his classmates.

Kurt definitely needed something to soothe him and Grunt had him try Percodan, one of the many system-derived painkillers. Before he knew it, Kurt found himself taking ten a day, so euphoric and relaxed did it make him feel. He almost began to *like* people.

Then, one summer night, Grunt and Kurt systemized themselves with heroin. Kurt thought he would never let himself get truly integrated, never become a real addict. He thought there wasn't enough system in Aberdeen for anyone to become hooked on it. What he didn't know was that all that Percodan he'd swallowed had been more than enough to systemize him. He had been fully integrated from the very first time he had taken it. He was wholly and utterly dependent on the system, though firmly convinced that he wasn't. It's quite normal for integratees to think they depend on nothing and nobody.

The ubiquity of the system did the rest.

He tried the system for the second time that same evening. He would have liked to lull himself to sleep with a nice piece of video, but he only had that film of the body snatchers, and he'd already seen it three times.

He decided to settle for a night of television instead.

The first item was a newscast, then came: a commercial break; the weather forecast for the next forty-eight hours; a game show whose rules he couldn't quite understand; a documentary on the sex life of tropical insects; more commercial breaks; some old film footage of gangsters starring James Cagney; a show where people argued; the fourth inning of a baseball game;

another newscast about sports events; a discussion show about incurable diseases; a show featuring a man with an ingratiating smile who talked about God and urged viewers to call a number that scrolled across the screen; another show with a young woman in her underclothes touching herself and panting who also urged viewers to call a number flashed up on the screen, which was not, however, the same number as the one recommended by the man with the ingratiating smile; one of those shows where people talk about their problems, that focused on a boy with a serious form of insomnia whom Homer would have phoned to advise him to try the system, had it not been for the fact that in that show there weren't any numbers displayed on the screen for you to call and that something warned him against talking to strangers about his relationship with the system.

Homer watched everything, rarely switching channels, and then only at the end of a show. He let himself be fascinated for hours by things that shouldn't have interested him much. It was a highly agreeable, contemplative passivity. This is another of the beneficial effects of the system: the attractiveness it imparts to things that are essentially stupid and boring.

There was no doubt, however, that a piece of quality film would have served his purpose better. He was almost sorry to waste his second systemization on such mediocre shows. He decided to go to Olympia the next day to join a video club that had a connoisseur-standard catalogue, with vintage film of hypothetical, extraordinary, not-scientifically-attested events. He would become a member and rent a few pieces of film, enough to last him at least a week. And with this reassuring thought he fell asleep.

86 The next morning he carried out his plan, overcoming his strong desire to go on sleeping. He went to the bus station, bought a ticket to Olympia, went to the video store, took out membership and left a deposit of twenty-five dollars. Half an hour later he was back out on the street with two large plastic bags containing a total of ten video recordings on magnetic tape of the following hypothetical, extraordinary, not-scientifically-attested events: the perfidy of a being from the planet Venus who entices a scientist with the promise of a long period of peace and prosperity; the traumatic experience of a quiet Californian family whose roof takes a direct hit from a wayward missile; the struggle between a gangster and a lawyer for the possession of the only woman left on Earth after a nuclear disaster; the reckless vanity of a woman who tries out an anti-wrinkle balsam based on certain enzymes and is turned into a

wasp; one of the various versions of the story of the scientist who invents an invisibility serum; the adventures of a man who agrees to test an experimental time machine, goes back into the past and decides to stay there because he meets the love of his life; the bloodlust of an entomologist's daughter who turns into a vampire butterfly at nightfall; the stratagem of an alien who installs himself in a man's mind with the aim of having him dominate the Earth on his behalf; the stubbornness of an engineer who builds an underwater house and moves into it with his whole family to prove to the world that it is not in the least dangerous; the effects of a surgical operation that enables a cretin to develop his intelligence to the point where he becomes a genius, falls in love with the woman doctor who has transformed him, but then starts to regress, little by little, till he turns back into the cretin he used to be.

Homer was satisfied, and convinced that he would have no problems systemizing himself for at least a week. On the first two days everything went as he had imagined: couch, inhalation, film, states of luminous warm contentment, drifting thoughts, phases when he hovered gently just above the state of drowsiness, and finally sleep, from which he would re-emerge around midday.

But on the third day, as he prepared to systemize himself for the fifth time in front of the pictures of the woman who is transformed into a wasp by the anti-wrinkle preparation, he had a shock. He was just extracting the requisite amount of system from the little bag, when he suddenly realized that the powder had almost run out. This shouldn't really have surprised him, because it was patently obvious that nothing that gets consumed can last for ever. Yet it had never even crossed his mind. He'd gone all the way to Olympia to rent those useless bits of vintage film while completely overlooking the most important fact, and now he found himself left with a dose of system that would barely be enough for that evening. He cursed himself roundly, slipped on his jacket and rushed to the North Aberdeen Bridge.

It was, as the saying goes, a dark and stormy night. An icy wind was blowing, and this seemed ominous. Kurt might have abandoned his camp under the bridge, the wind seemed to moan. What would Homer do if he had? Who could he turn to? He might be a novice as far as the system was concerned, but he already sensed that the whole business moved along secret channels that were a complete mystery to him. Even he could see that entering the system was not as simple as subscribing to a cable TV channel.

Please heaven, let him not have gone away, Homer implored as he ran. Please heaven, he repeated, peering to see if any human shape was moving in the darkness under the bridge.

'Kurt...' he said in a small voice, when he realized that there was nothing under the bridge except the darkness and the brushwood waving in the icy wind and the rotten planks of the bridge and the storm-ruffled water and a can of sausages which Homer retrieved from the grass, on the spot where Kurt's camp had been until a few days before.

He fell to the ground and lay there on his back, gazing up at the planks of the bridge and listening to the Antarctic howl of the wind and the endlessly murmuring river. It came home to Homer just how alone he was in the world and he screamed long and loud into the night.

Another question: What do people get out of the system?

Answer: First, a sense of calm and solace. Secondly, a general elevation of their moral and intellectual inclinations, a heightening of the finest mental qualities, an ardent afflatus of goodwill toward others, an urge to do great, noble, charitable deeds, a higher spirit of self-sacrifice, increased self-confidence, and a clearer awareness of their own resources. And it should not be imagined that this awareness is simply a delusion caused by the hot, white light of the system, for within the system the mental, imaginative and emotional faculties are elevated to the highest degree.

In short, during those brief moments when the light of the system illuminates the individual in full splendor, that individual is in effect a new and better human being.

The only problem is what happens *outside* the system, especially when the light is turned off.

He forced himself not to panic. Aberdeen was not a big place, after all. He calmed himself with the thought that if he asked around he'd find him in the end. The only problem was that he didn't have many close friends whom he could ask for information. Correction: he didn't have *any* close friends. During those eighteen years of sleeplessness he had lived like a recluse. He had limited his contacts with human beings to unavoidable occasions, like when he went to the store to buy food and those consumer items known as 'household products'. He also went to the Laundromat, and to the post office to send his space toys to the nostalgia geeks. Otherwise, apart from his rare trips to Olympia, his only outings were those long walks in the woods.

He worried that the few people he could ask almost certainly saw him as a friendless loner and that their suspicions would be aroused if he suddenly showed an interest in another human being. They might think he was some kind of hobo-killing maniac and call the police; so he had better tread carefully.

The next morning he was preparing to go to the post office to send one of his packages. As he did so, it occurred to him that this would be a good opportunity to ask for information without attracting too much attention. He could strike up a conversation with the clerk, make a bit of small talk – as one does in such situations – and casually ask, I wonder what happened to that guy who used to camp under the bridge?

There was only one flaw in this plan, namely his total lack of experience in making small talk. Still, he told himself that he would improvise on the spur of the moment and that he would think of something to say if he really had to.

Emboldened, he prepared the package and went straight to the post office. But when he entered, the clerk seemed lost in thought, and showed no sign of reacting in his usual manner. His usual reaction, when he saw Homer arrive with one of his packages, was to burst into laughter, raise his hand, crook his forefinger and say, in a hoarse, broken voice, 'Ho-mer... Ho-mer...' in what was supposed to be a poignant impression of ET. Then he would laugh again with an exaggerated gusto that reminded Homer of the canned laughter in TV sitcoms. He just couldn't understand why this guy was so amused by his little act, especially as he'd been performing it for years. Maybe this is the meaning of life, Homer mused. But if so, it was a meaning Homer could not fathom.

Still, at least it didn't irritate him anymore. Besides, it was his own fault, in a way, for yielding to the clerk's curiosity.

'All very mysterious,' the clerk had said on one of Homer's visits.

'Huh?' Homer had muttered.

'All these packages...'

'What about them?'

'Rather unusual, isn't it?'

'I sell toy flying saucers by mail order,' Homer had replied, gruffly.

The clerk had pondered this for a while, then said: 'Toy flying saucers, eh?'

'Yeah.'

'And you sell them by mail order?'

'Yeah.'

'Well, we'd better send this by intergalactic express, then.'

Homer had given him a dirty look, but he'd persisted: 'Yeah, we'd better make it an intergalactic express delivery. Can't keep them aliens waiting, can we?' Another long burst of sitcom laughter followed.

Homer had given him a truly filthy look, but to no avail. The darker his scowl, the more the guy laughed. He went on laughing as he filled out the appropriate form, and didn't stop till he'd tossed Homer's package into the registered mail basket behind him. Homer paid and went out, wondering whether it would be any use writing an anonymous letter to the US Postmaster General to demand that the clerk be fired.

From that time on it was pure hell. As soon as Homer stepped through the door of the post office the clerk would start his ET impression. He'd crook his forefinger, point it toward Homer, and away he'd go.

But that day, when Homer was hoping to strike up a conversation and ask about Kurt, the clerk gave not the slightest sign of recognition. He just sat there impassively, waiting for Homer to give him the package. He didn't say a word as he filled out the form and stamped it. The silence paralyzed Homer. Shit, he thought, this can't be happening.

He opened his mouth and muttered something, but the clerk didn't seem to understand, because he stared at him blankly. Homer wondered if he'd turned into a triffid. Dazed, he paid the postage and walked toward the exit, trying to keep his composure. He was on the point of opening the door when he heard the clerk's voice: 'Ho-mer. . .'

'Yeah?' he said, turning around.

'*Brrzhypsoln kahss Heewox,* Ho-mer,' said the clerk in his ET voice.

Homer went out, angry and disconsolate. The clerk's laughter echoed in his ears all the way home.

Another question, which is simply the previous one from a different point of view: What does the system give people?

Answer: water, sugar, protein, vegetable fats, rubber, ammonia, resin, latex, lactic acid, sulphuric acid and meconic acid, as well as various alkaloids including morphine (ten to fifteen per cent), papaverine (one to three per cent), thebaine (one to two per cent), codeine (one to four per cent) and noscapine (four to eight per cent). That is what the opium system contains in its natural state. As we have already seen, however, in order for the system to achieve maximum effectiveness certain crucial alterations need to be made which mother nature was unwilling, or unable, to make herself.

After his complete failure to get any information at the post office, Homer grew pessimistic about his chances of ever finding Kurt. He abandoned the idea of making a similar attempt with the storekeeper, because the man wasn't very communicative at the best of times, and his behavior was extremely erratic. If the post office clerk had behaved so unpredictably, there was no knowing what that guy might do.

There's just no trusting human beings, he thought. Difference is always lying in wait. That the clerk had behaved so differently on this day of all days was suspicious, to say the least. It was also very odd that Kurt – his only point of contact with that wonderful alternative world – had vanished so soon after Homer's integration into the system. He had no proof, of course, but all the signs were that the differents were carrying out a concerted plan to block the escape route he'd finally discovered after all these years.

When evening fell, another doubt struck him: was he still under the protection of the system, or would he have to stay awake again as he had for the past eighteen years? He went out for a stroll among the trees. It'll clear my head, he told himself. But what he was really trying to do was drive those unpleasant thoughts out of his mind. He wished he could have those airy thoughts that came to him when he system-ized himself, thoughts that wafted him clear of the force of gravity, like the gentle lifting of a hot-air balloon. He walked for hours, but it was to no avail, because his ideas became increasingly confused and tangled. Unpleasant thoughts multiplied like rabbits, and it was a miracle that he didn't fall to the ground, dragged down by the weight inside him.

Eventually he turned homeward, almost resigned to another long period of forced sleeplessness. His path took him past the Public Library, and he remembered the time when he'd worked there as night janitor. He thought back wistfully to those days and sighed. But just as he reached his own front door, having left behind him the library and the memories it had re-awoken, he remembered something Kurt had said that fateful night. He'd said that he often went to the library and that he liked writers beginning with B.

Homer glimpsed a ray of hope. He inhaled what was left of the powdered system and watched the film of the woman being transformed into a wasp by the anti-wrinkle cream, and the more the minutes passed the more that question of writers beginning with B seemed the right trail to follow, and in this new flush of optimism he fell asleep, long before the film of the wasp-woman had ended.

The next morning he knew what to do. He went to the Public Library and scanned the relevant shelf. He was surprised to see how many writers' names began with the same letter. This complicated matters, for even supposing Kurt read all the writers beginning with B, and even assuming he managed to read a book a day – a pretty optimistic assumption given his lifestyle – there were still far too many books. It might be months before he received the message that Homer was planning to send him.

He could put a message in every one of the books, but that would greatly increase the risk of someone else reading it, and that might be dangerous. It was a risk he couldn't afford to take. So there was no alternative. He must immediately hit on a book that Kurt would definitely read and – equally important – read soon. As he scanned the rows of titles on the shelves of the letter B, the plan that had appeared to be so simple the previous night seemed unexpectedly complicated.

There was a *Wuthering Heights*, a *Splendors and Miseries of Courtesans*, a *Heart of a Dog*, a *Clockwork Orange*, a *Master and Margarita*, a *Sleepwalkers*, a *Watt*, an *End of the Road*, a *Snow White*, a *Forest in the Night*, a *Reckoning*, a *Martian Chronicles* and even an *And Where Were You, Adam?*, which Homer thought a pretty weird title for a book.

Despair had almost reduced him to choosing a book at random, when his eye fell on *The Soft Machine*, by a certain William S. Burroughs. That wasn't a bad title. There were another couple of books by the same writer which also had good titles: *The Ticket that Exploded* and *Naked Lunch*. But Homer focused on *The Soft Machine*; he liked it because it reminded him of hot-air balloons and of the airy thoughts he had when he systemized himself. Yes, that was exactly how the system worked. Like a soft machine.

Feeling inspired, he went straight to the request counter, filled out the form, returned home with the book, opened it at the first page and wrote his message for Kurt. He used a pencil, because he had a certain respect for books. The message was: 'I'm so tired I can't sleep'. He was sure Kurt would understand it.

When it came to adding his signature, however, he hesitated, because Kurt never seemed to remember his real name. In the end, somewhat reluctantly, he wrote 'Boddah', adding his phone number. As he walked back toward the library to return the book, he thought about the way he had relinquished his name, wondering whether he ought to feel ashamed. Isn't it like relinquishing a part of yourself? he wondered. And he wondered whether there was some obscure reason why Kurt persisted in calling him Boddah. At first sight it seemed perfectly natural: Kurt called him Boddah because that had been his best friend's name. It was even rather flattering, in a way: it meant he reminded Kurt of this friend whom he remembered so fondly.

What worried Homer was the fact that Boddah didn't exist. How could he possibly remind Kurt of someone who didn't exist? What could he possibly have in common with Boddah, if there had never *been* a Boddah? In logical terms, if A must be followed by B, there is only one thing you can have in common with something that doesn't exist. Homer decided he would rather not think about that something, even in hypothetical terms. He consoled himself with the thought that it was perfectly normal to relinquish a little of yourself when you agree to integrate yourself into a system.

Besides, who said being real was the only way of existing in this world?

He quickened his pace and began to breathe harder. His breath turned to clouds of vapor in the cold air, and the sound he made was like the pistons of a soft machine.

Things happened that were shown on television.

The entire crew of an American space shuttle died in an explosion seventy-four seconds after lift-off; seventy other citizens died in a discotheque in West Berlin as a result of a bomb blast; a commission appointed by the Department of Justice decreed that certain pornographic publications were potentially harmful and might induce American citizens to behave violently toward women and children; the President signed a reform of the fiscal law whereby taxes were reduced for all taxpayers, especially those in the higher income brackets; more than twenty thousand cases of a new virus that caused immune deficiency were recorded, most of them concerning American citizens who had already died, and it was predicted that fatalities would increase tenfold in the next five years; American citizens bought sixteen million cars, of which only twenty-eight per cent were imported; and there was a nuclear accident in a small town in the Soviet Union, in which, thank the Lord, no American citizen was involved.

Things also happened that were not shown on television. A little girl with freckles stroked a gray cat; an elm tree was struck by lightning; a truck driver spent the night in a motel and fell asleep thinking about what he used to think when he was twenty; a cloud of moths gathered under the light of a streetlamp; a woman made love to a man in exchange for fifty dollars; a nine-year-old boy thought he was immortal; two people quarreled and stopped greeting one another when they met; a girl pushed her hair out of her eyes; an astrologer foretold the future to a terminally ill patient, and a cash register tinkled, while, outside the store, night was falling.

And while all these things were happening, time passed and 1986 drew to a close. The message that Homer had left in the soft-machine book remained unanswered. Homer had sadly returned to his old life of packages to be sent off, walks in the woods, sleepless nights and little else. When he was at home – which was most of the time – he tried not to stray too far from the phone, but the phone never rang. He even bought himself an answering machine for the times when he had to go out, even though he suspected that Kurt wasn't the kind of person who left messages, and Homer didn't have much confidence in the gadget anyway.

It hardly ever stopped raining, and on the rare occasions when it did stop, the sky was so gray that it would probably have been better if it had just gone on raining. Homer tried to imagine the reason for Kurt's silence. He trusted him and couldn't believe that he had left him alone, bereft of system and doomed to sleeplessness. Sometimes he feared that something serious might have happened to him, but he banished the thought from his mind and carried on. He preferred to think Kurt was lying low to keep out of the way of the differents. This idea found some support in a spate of graffiti that had begun to appear on the streets of Aberdeen. They were different from the premonitory scrawls that had led him to Kurt a year earlier. Their messages were even weirder. They said things like

AMPUTATE ACROBATS

or

THE SUN SETS TOO

or

BOAT AKK

But the handwriting seemed the same, and Homer became increasingly convinced that they were Kurt's work. This in turn made him wonder whether one of them was a coded message to him, and he spent hours trying to decrypt them. He searched for anagrams and read the messages from back to front. He replaced the letters with numbers which he then tried to phone, and when the prerecorded voice of the operator told him that the number he had dialed was not correct or had been deactivated, then, instead of checking the number and trying to dial it again as the operator advised, he replaced the letters with symbols and other letters, using every method he could think of. But all he produced was a set of even more incomprehensible messages which began to sound as outlandish as the clerk's words on Homer's last visit to the post office. Things like

EEZH = KYWTT OOX

or

MK ^{SYSTEM} YT

or

o . . . oooz⊖?

He had reduced language to gibberish; words had lost all meaning. And when after a while even the graffiti stopped appearing, he just gave up. He didn't even have anything to decipher now. Even that faint trace of Kurt's existence had been taken from him. Homer feared Kurt might have fallen into the hands of the differents and be lost forever.

In a sense this was true. Kurt had been caught scrawling BOAT PEOPLE GO HOME on the wall of the local YMCA.

The judge didn't see the point of the message but recognized the style. It showed the same taste for the absurd as the other graffiti scattered around town. He concluded that they were all Kurt's work and sentenced him to clean them off.

As soon as he'd finished his sentence, Kurt started

all over again, but this time was caught at once. He was standing in an alley, facing the wall of a bank, with a red marker in his hand, when a police patrol car arrived and caught him in its headlamps. They drove him to the police station, took his fingerprints and made him write a kind of confession.

'Tonight,' runs the text of the confession, 'I was in an alley behind the SeaFirst Bank and I scrawled some graffiti on the wall of the bank. I don't know why I did it, but I did. I now realize that it's stupid to do that kind of thing and I'm sorry and I apologize. I also admit dropping my red marker on the ground when I saw the police car turning into the alley. I did that because I intended to deny that it had been me who had scrawled on the wall of the Seafirst Bank. That was another really stupid thing to do, because they might have accused an innocent person instead of me and that wouldn't have been right. I apologize for that as well.'

Homer had no way of knowing all this. All he knew was that Kurt had disappeared, and with him the graffiti on the walls around town. So his life moved along to the same rhythm as before. Time marched doggedly onward, without having a clear idea of where it was going. Kurt and his system had vanished as suddenly as they had appeared, into the realms of an uncertain past, the past where things may or may not have happened.

Homer reverted to type. Obsessed by the difference of the townsfolk, he walked the streets warily, trudging along with a stony expression on his face. The smokestack of the Rayonier continued to belch out its columns of smoke, what remained of the souls of the chopped-down trees. Homer was his old self again. Just plain Homer. All trace of Boddah had gone.

He even stopped cracking his knuckles. And he stopped watching film of extraordinary, hypothetical, not-scientifically-attested events. He used the television like a radio. He'd prepare the packets of space-ships, lunar tractors and space guns with the TV chattering away in the background. When he heard the canned laughter of the sitcoms he got so furious he could have wept, or smashed a flying saucer on the head of one of the geeks who sent him those creepy letters. How he hated those letters! He burned every one of them as soon as he'd taken note of its order, as if the paper it was written on was the carrier of some incurable disease.

He could have turned the TV off, it's true. But for some reason he couldn't bring himself to do it, and however much the canned laughter upset him, he preferred it to the silence that enveloped his motionless house. It was a silence of far-off noises – a car engine fading into the distance, a woman's voice calling out somewhere, the low electric hum of the fridge which would sometimes, without warning, become as sharp as a newly honed knife.

Things would have gone on like this indefinitely, had Homer not decided to relieve the endless misery of his sleepless nights by reading the occasional book. He had never been a great reader, and he hadn't opened a book in years. Books were full of stories, and he couldn't see the point of stories. He couldn't understand what practical usefulness there was in learning what had happened to people he didn't know who lived in places he would never go to. There was another thing that bothered him, too – the fact that in the stories in books something was always on the point of happening whereas in his life nothing ever happened. Yes, he thought books were implausible for precisely that reason, because something always happened. Reality was different: there you are, waiting for something to happen, hoping for something to happen, but it never does. Like this matter of Kurt's disappearance: if he'd been a character in a book, something would have happened. You would have read how Homer spent his nights shuffling and replacing letters to decrypt the messages written on the walls of the streets till he was worn out. You would have read how, when he was on the point of giving up, his eyes bloodshot and sunken in their purple sockets, he suddenly, for no particular reason, began to do a first degree equation – he, who didn't even know what a first-degree equation was – and hit on the solution, worked out Kurt's telephone number and called him, and it all started again, powdered system, film, sleeping and all. Or perhaps the story would have been simpler: you would have read how months later, when Homer had stopped thinking about it – though the very idea of him ceasing to think about a system that enabled him to sleep is completely absurd – he just happened to bump into Kurt somewhere, at the post office, say, where he, Homer, was sending his usual space-toy package and he, Kurt, was sending... sending... well, never mind what Kurt was sending, it doesn't matter what he was sending, because the important thing was that they, Homer and Kurt, met up again, and that after all those months everything started over as before, and so on and so forth.

But since neither Homer nor Kurt was a character in a book and Aberdeen was not a place in a book, none of these things, nor anything remotely resembling them, had happened and everything had started over as before, yes, but *before* before, the before that should no longer have existed, the before that you never find in books, because stories in books consist of nothing but afters, after this and after that; the before that things revert to when nothing happens.

Nevertheless, despite his mistrust of the way the stories in books entwined and unraveled themselves, Homer started going to the Public Library and borrowing books, and reading them on his walks in the woods or during his visits to the Laundromat, while he was waiting for the washing machine to complete its cycle. At first he found it an effort. The words he read in books got stuck in his mind, blocking the path of the ones he should have read on the next line. He saw words as autonomous, significant units, and certain allusive turns of phrase, certain vague, ambiguous things, things left unsaid or up in the air, made him uneasy. Then he started reading more submissively and tried to accept the possibility that words might not be autonomous or significant. He tried to enjoy the way things happened in books, and although in his life there was still absolutely nothing happening, the distinction between the inverosimilitude of books and the reality of things no longer seemed so clear-cut to him. He also noticed that in books fewer things happened than one might think; in fact, in some books almost nothing happened at all, just as in his life. And yet, even in the absence of any events, books always seemed full of things. Homer couldn't understand this; and he couldn't understand how the stories that appeared on TV were not equally full, though some of them, such as the news and the talk shows, were undoubtedly true. He couldn't understand why the canned laughter of the sitcoms plunged him into a state of suffocating despair, while the far more depressing stories of the characters in certain books saddened him in a very different and even pleasurable way.

Perhaps this was due to the hypnotic influence of the words. Once he read a book about the difficulties a man encountered in gaining access to a castle. The book began like this: 'It was late in the evening when K. arrived. The village was deep in snow.' When he reached the period after the word 'snow', Homer had stopped, content. He liked the idea of the village deep in snow, though he hadn't formed any image in his mind either of the village itself or of how it might have sunk into the snow. He also liked the beginning of another, much older book, particularly the phrase 'darkness was upon the face of the deep'. And he liked the end of a book that had been left unfinished, 'a willful convulsion of brute nature. . .'

One day it occurred to him to check the books by writers beginning with B and he borrowed the one where he had left his message for Kurt several months before, the soft-machine book. The librarian handed it to him, and he turned at once to the page where he had written that he was so tired he couldn't sleep. His penciled words signed 'Boddah' were still there; no one had erased them, no one had added anything. No one had even opened the book since then, he suspected. He returned the book to the librarian, muttering that he had made a mistake, and left. Outside, needless to say, it was raining. Homer set off for home, feeling utterly disheartened, drained of all motivation and hope. After twenty yards he stopped. How could he face the four walls of home in that dejected state? He decided to go to the post office to check his mailbox. He entered as quietly as possible, hoping the clerk wouldn't notice him. He couldn't face his ET act today. Luckily there were a couple of people in a line partly blocking his view; if he walked straight past, with his head bowed, toward the wall of mailboxes, perhaps he would be able to collect his mail and leave without having to endure the usual torture. Everything seemed to be going smoothly, but just as he was closing the box, in his anxiety to be quick, he dropped the keys, and their impact on the ground produced a sound wave that echoed with unusual intensity just when the post office happened to be suspended in a microsecond of total silence. The people in the line turned toward Homer and the rustle of their clothes made the clerk look up from the form he was stamping. Homer and the clerk stared at one another in silence. The people in the line stared at the keys that had fallen on the floor. The only sound was the patter of the rain. Everything was still, as at the beginning of the gunfight scene in Westerns. Homer bent down to pick up the keys, watched by the people in the line and the clerk. Nothing happened. Nobody said a word. The only hint of a reaction was an imperceptible movement of the clerk's lips. Homer had the impression that it was a sort of smirk, but the movement was too brief for him to be sure. What was certain was the fact that the clerk lowered his head and resumed stamping his form. As if in response to a command, the people in the line turned around, losing all interest in Homer and his keys. The patter of the rain seemed to recede into the background, and with it the stillness of the scene. Everything returned to normal; everyone minded their own business, even the clerk appeared to be engrossed in his forms. Homer closed the mailbox and scuttled out like a fleeing cockroach. Once out on the street he heaved a sigh of relief at having got away with it for once. The tension had been so great that he'd almost forgotten how dejected he'd been until a few minutes earlier. Now he could go home, he thought to himself. But just as he was about to examine the two envelopes he had found in the box, an unpleasant thought struck him. What was behind the clerk's behavior? Never before had that son of a bitch failed to mock him. Sometimes he had pretended to spare him or not to recognize him or not to notice him enter the office, but at the last moment, just when Homer's brain was daring to form the idea that he had got away with it, the clerk's routine would begin. Why hadn't it done so today? Why had he merely stared at him like that, given just the faintest of smiles, which perhaps had only existed in Homer's imagination? All these questions were destined to remain unanswered, he realized that. So he began instead to examine the two envelopes that he had found in the mailbox, trying to banish those gnawing doubts, without wholly succeeding. One of the letters was from his first customer, the Jim who had been DESPERATELY seeking the Yonezawa Moon Explorer. He wrote every week and Homer always instantly recognized his stiff, shaky, manic-depressive's handwriting, without even having to read the sender's name on the envelope. Jim was extremely persistent, and took liberties that infuriated Homer. He was always asking him for a phone number where he

could call him, or urging him to have a fax installed to speed up their correspondence, or telling him about some meeting of space-toy fans where it would be great to have Homer among the participants. Once he had even taken the unheard-of step of asking if he could visit him at home so that he could admire just a few of the treasures – as Jim called them – that Homer kept hidden away there. All these suggestions fell on deaf ears. Homer simply sent him his weekly package with a letter as unvarying as a pre-printed form. Dear Jim, Thank you for your check for ___ dollars. I enclose the ___ which you ordered. Sincerely yours, H.A. He always signed with his initials alone because these guys were obsessives; they'd be quite capable of knocking on the door of every Alienson in the State of Washington and Oregon too till they tracked him down. As for Jim's suggestions, Homer never once

responded to them. Jim was certainly a good customer, because he sent him seven or eight hundred
dollars' worth of checks a month, but the mere idea
that a person like that existed on the face of the earth
put Homer in a state of uncontrollable irritation.
There were days when he felt so exasperated by Jim's
pushiness that as soon as he recognized his handwriting he tore up the envelope without even opening it;
and he did so on that day too, because he couldn't face
reading it, and anyway, before the week was out, not
having received a reply, Jim was bound to send him
another even more irksome missive.

So he was left with just one envelope in his hand.
This one was more puzzling. The handwriting didn't
seem to be that of any of his usual customers, yet it
reminded him of something that he couldn't bring
clearly into focus. This was a day of indecipherable
events. Thoughtfully, he turned the envelope over and
over in his hands. The sender's name was not given,
but when his eye fell on the postmark he noticed that
the letter had been sent from Aberdeen. He had never
sold a single space toy in Aberdeen. He was standing
on the street, the rain was falling and a truck had just
gone by with its load of logs on the way to the highway;
across the street a redneck logger in a fisherman's

cape had thrown him a sidelong glance and kept on walking; the hardware store to his right was deserted, and a few yards ahead there was a parking meter which looked as if some drunk had taken an ax to it. Who could have written to him from a place like this? He opened the envelope, using a key as a paper knife. And when he read what was written inside he realized at once who could. The letter was from someone who wanted to shoot himself with an atomic disintegrator and wondered if Boddah happened to have anything in that line. The letter ended with an address. And it wasn't hard to guess who, and what, he would find at that number on East Second Street, was it, Boddah?

3.

High There

At around the time when the question of love made its appearance, Homer B. Alienson imagined giving a television interview about his experience of integration into the system and other details connected with that experience, such as his friendship with Kurt. Never having made even the most fleeting of appearances on any kind of screen, let alone an imaginary one, Homer saw no reason to decline the invitation. It was a show with very low audience figures – with no audience figures at all, to be perfectly honest, since the entire show, and the network that was to air it, only existed in Homer's systemized mind.

'So everything started over where it had left off?' said the talk-show hostess when Homer had finished telling the story of the letter sent from Aberdeen.

'Huh?' said Homer, not sure that he had understood the question.

'What I meant, Mr Alienson, was that I suppose you went to see who lived at that address on East Second Street?'

'Sure, I went there,' said Homer.

'And the person who lived at that address in East Second Street was your hobo friend, am I right?'

'My what friend?'

'Your friend Kurt, Mr Alienson. The person who initiated you into the system.'

'Oh,' said Homer. He breathed in air through his nose, trying to clear from his nostrils the residue of the extra-large dose of powdered system that he'd inhaled before the recording began.

'Well, Mr Alienson?'

'Yeah,' said Homer, 'it was Kurt.' And he remembered the times when he used to go over to Kurt's house, as he did whenever he was running out of powdered system, though often he went over just for the sake of going there, because he eventually got into the habit of visiting Kurt even when he didn't need anything.

Partly because of the problem of the differents, and partly because of his own character, which made contact with other human beings an effort, Homer had never had any friends. But at Kurt's place things were easier. He could squat down on the floor somewhere, clear himself a space among the empty beer cans and the beer glasses crammed with ash and cigarette butts, and sit there for hours without having to say a word. There were often a lot of other people around, harmless people, who had nothing to do with 'difference'; guys who drank beer, put on loud, really loud music, and experimented with all kinds of systems, which ranged from smoking a vegetable nick-named Affy Bud to inhaling the propellant gas from cans of shaving cream. Homer never joined in the activities of the house, preferring to remain aloof in his corner, a mute, passive spectator. He discovered that he enjoyed watching what others did, while his ears buzzed from the deafening volume of the music and his mouth filled with the unmistakable, bitter taste of the powdered system that he inhaled in the bathroom.

'Tell us about your friend's house, Mr Alienson,' said the talk-show hostess, snapping Homer out of his reverie.

'What do you want to know?'

'Well, was there anything that particularly struck you about it?'

'It stank.'

'What of?'

'Kurt said it was rat piss, but it was really turtle shit.'

'Turtle excrement?' she echoed, to remind him that they were on TV, even if it was only imaginary TV.

'He liked turtles. He bought a few and put them in the lounge, in a sort of makeshift terrarium that discharged the water and the sh... ah... the excrement into the foundations of the house through a hole in the floor. But the house was a dump; the wood was so rotten that the water seeped up through the floorboards. That's why it stank.'

'I see,' said the hostess, her face an inscrutable mask.

'He said he liked turtles because they had a "fuck-you" attitude.'

She made a strange gesture with her hand, as if to smooth her hair back over her ear. Homer had the impression that she was trying to tell him something.

'What's the problem? Aren't I supposed to say "fuck you" on TV? Is that it?'

She stiffened and gave a forced smile. 'Well, I'd rather you didn't, but if you really can't avoid it...'

'I just wanted to tell it like it was,' he defended himself.

'Yes, I appreciate that. Now, could we please move on?'

Homer had the impression that the talk-show hostess did not merely consider him a fool, but would gladly have throttled him for the way he was ruining the show. He thought of pointing out that this was the first time he'd been on TV, but arguing that, despite that, he didn't see any harm in saying such things. Then he thought better of it, and went on with his account of the turtles.

'The idea is that turtles hate people and that that's why they retreat into their shells, it's their way of giving people the finger.'

The hostess raised her eyebrows.

'Anyway, there's not much they can do with that shell on their backs,' Homer went on.

'Isn't there?'

'No, because it's really their spine.'

'I see,' said the hostess, tightening her lips.

'People think the shell protects them, but it doesn't. Have you ever tried hitting a turtle on its back?'

'No, I don't believe I ever have tried that,' she replied, rolling her eyes skyward – metaphorically speaking, of course, since they were indoors.

'I thought not. Otherwise you'd have known that if you knock on the shell it hurts them.'

'That's fascinating, Mr Alienson,' said the hostess,

though her tone suggested that she was dying to get off the subject. But Homer was too engrossed in his story to notice.

'And if they fall on their back, it splits open and they die,' he announced with great solemnity.

'Is that a fact?' The hostess was the picture of despair. An entire show trashed by an idiot.

'Yeah. It's like they had their spine on the outside.'

She stared at him and said nothing. If she kept quiet, maybe this fool would stop driveling about turtles. Homer sighed. She parted her lips and sat motionless, waiting.

'It was Kurt who explained that to me. He's really into turtles.'

A commercial break intervened. When they came back on air the hostess quickly changed the subject.

'Now, then, Mr Alienson, can you tell us what your friend Kurt was doing at the time?'

Homer thought for a while before answering. His memory had been playing tricks with him lately and the rectilinear logic of the past, the logic that proceeded from all of those yesterdays to today, sometimes coiled back on itself, assuming curious spiral forms more similar to the contortedness of some of his thoughts than to the normal image of the concept of time. For a moment he wondered whether the system could alter the course of time, slow it down, impede it, bring it to a halt, so that the days, instead of passing by as they are generally thought to do, rammed into the back of each other in a gigantic pile-up. Homer, at the wheel of a car which he did not in fact possess, a 1990 Present convertible, had stopped in the middle of the carriageway for no apparent reason and sat there in the driving seat blithely contemplating that point on the horizon where the two sides of the highway converged, an illusory denial of the Euclidean principle that parallel lines only meet at infinity. At one time the inverted V of the asphalt strip that was framed in the rectangle of the windshield would have been like a wedge of anxiety driven into his heart, would have represented the future, the future that he couldn't know but that he felt he could do without, a future of sinister uncertainty that he hoped he would never have to reach but toward which he was forced to travel because of the cars that harried him from behind, an ever-rising river of bygone days, a honking past that wouldn't let him rest. But since he had become integrated into the system and had started sleeping like a 'normal' human being again, the Present car in which he was driving had stalled without warning, whereupon the car of the day before, unable to brake in time, had crashed into the back of him, followed in succession by the car of the day before yesterday and those of the days before that. Homer continued to contemplate the sweet fixity of a future which had at last stopped drawing nearer, as he enjoyed the sound of time crashing into itself, a sound that grew fainter as the pile-up of days lengthened, until it became a sonic vibration poised between the imperceptible and the imaginary world of the things we *think* we hear, as remote as the voice of the talk-show hostess who now, or so it seemed to him, kept repeating 'Mr Alienson?' in a vain attempt to elicit an answer to her question.

What the hell did she want? His memories were already pretty confused and if she kept pressuring him he might not be able to focus on anything. He remembered that Kurt had shared his shack with another guy, who worked as a cabinet maker and played in a rock band. His name was Matt and it was him who invited all those other guys over. If Matt had had his way, life would have been one long party, but Kurt didn't care for that kind of thing. He was the quiet type, and the fewer people there were around the better, as far as he was concerned. He would have liked just to be on his own and play guitar – he was very fond of playing guitar – but that wasn't possible.

One day, in desperation, Kurt took a roll of colored packing tape and stretched it across the floor. A red line now divided the apartment in two.

'This side of the tape is my part of the house. The other side's yours,' he said to Matt. 'From now on, you and your friends keep to your part and don't come and bother me in mine.'

The plan seemed workable, until one of Matt's friends pointed out that they'd have to cross the red line to get to the bathroom.

'Fuck you,' said Kurt. 'You can go and piss out in the yard. The bathroom's on my side.'

There was always something worrying Kurt. If it wasn't Matt's friends coming round to booze, it was his terror that the landlady might phone to remind him of the rent he owed or the fact that he was broke and had to live on rice and fries. He thought he was going to die of hunger any day or that he might have to go back to sleeping under the bridge.

Once, while he was making fries, he burned his hand. It was a severe burn and for a while it looked like he'd never play guitar again.

'He worked in a hotel in Ocean Shores, a holiday

resort near here, about twenty miles from Aberdeen,' Homer said at length.

'What did he do there?'

'He was the maintenance man. He did the cleaning, straightened up the rooms.' He omitted to mention that Kurt spent most of the time locked in one of the unoccupied rooms sleeping in front of the television. He also neglected to say that Kurt was always looking for cheap ways of systemizing himself because he was perennially short of money. He tried alternative but ineffective solutions like drinking cough syrup. When things got really bad, Homer would sell a couple more toys and give Kurt the money to buy some good stuff. He felt morally obliged to help him; if it hadn't been for Kurt he would never have gotten into the system.

'What did he do in his spare time?' asked the hostess.

'At weekends he went to Olympia, which is an artistic town, full of imaginative people. He liked it better than Aberdeen, though even there he didn't really fit in.'

'Why not?'

'The kids in Olympia had created a world of their own and played a kind of music they called love rock. They wanted to achieve a state of childlike innocence, but without entering the system. Kurt called them 'the

Calvinists', because they all dressed like their leader, a guy called Calvin. They had short hair, whereas Kurt had been growing his long.' And not washing it, he added in his thoughts, preferring to omit this detail from his story. Something made him mistrust the talk-show hostess and the whole situation he was in. 'What Kurt liked about the Calvinists was that they made him look back on his own childhood.' After a short pause, he added, with a final flourish: 'He had a K tattooed on his arm, too. So he wouldn't forget he'd been a child once.'

The hostess gave him a what-the-fuck-are-you-talking-about-now kind of look. Homer noticed and hastened to explain. 'A K inside a shield. It was the logo of K Records, the Calvinists' label.'

'I see,' said the hostess, who in fact saw very little but decided not to pursue the matter. She didn't want to get embroiled in another embarrassing and untelevisual situation like that of the turtles. 'And how long did he stay in this shack on East Second Street?'

'Who, Kurt?'

The hostess sighed. 'Yes, Kurt.'

'He was evicted two months later.'

Two months later than what, you fuckwit? thought the hostess, but kept that thought to herself.

'He hadn't paid the rent,' Homer went on, nodding his head solemnly.

'So where did he go?'

'Let me think.'

'Think away, but try not to be too long about it.'

'He moved to Olympia, as far as I recall. Yeah, that's right. He moved in with Tracy.'

'Tracy?'

'North Pear Street,' squeaked Homer triumphantly, piercing the studio's microphones. 'See? I even remembered the address.'

'Tra-cy?' the hostess repeated through gritted teeth.

'Kurt's girlfriend. He'd started seeing a girl, believe it or not. His first serious girlfriend. Tracy.'

She was the ideal girlfriend for Kurt – a year older than him, and sexually experienced. She showed him what it really meant to be with a woman. Her eyes were large and brown, her hair dark, her body soft and curvy. She knew even more about music than he did, because she'd been to hundreds of punk-rock shows.

Kurt had a hard time believing that a girl actually liked him, and this caused a few problems at first. But Tracy told him she'd love him so much that all his fears and self-doubts would disappear. Kurt said: 'Okay, let's give it a try.'

'So he decided to live like a civilized person,' the talk-show hostess suggested.

'Well, no; to be honest, his life there wasn't much different from the way it had been in Aberdeen,' said Homer. 'It was full of animals.'

'What was?'

'Their apartment.'

'Animals.'

'Yeah. Ah... let me see. There were two rabbits, three cats, a few rats... I can't remember exactly how many rats, I'm sorry. Maybe it'll come to me.'

'Never mind,' said the hostess, shifting uncomfortably in her seat.

'Then there were a lot of flies, and Chim-Chim the monkey.'

'Chim-Chim the monkey,' the hostess echoed him in a faraway voice.

'He was made of plastic, though.'

'The monkey.'

'Yeah. He was very fond of Chim-Chim. He used to call him his most prized possession.'

'The plastic monkey.'

'The house was pretty smelly. It mainly smelled of rat piss.' The hostess's jaw dropped. 'Oh, and I was forgetting,' Homer added.

'Yes?' said the hostess, as if she'd just awoken from a trance.

'The turtles. I was forgetting them. There were turtles too.'

At the sound of the word 'turtles' the hostess went rather obviously weak at the knees and the studio assistant hastily gave the signal for a commercial. During the break Homer thought about the apartment in Olympia, the smell, the animals that lived there, the flies, and the fly-strips that hung from the ceiling. He saw in his mind the incredible number of objects that filled it, dusty broken objects that Kurt and Tracy bought in thrift stores. He remembered the huge poster of a rock band whose name he couldn't remember, the sketches by Kurt hanging on the walls, the paintings of distended fetuses adrift in hostile landscapes, imprisoned in forests of black trees with gnarled branches, the self-portraits with their acid colors, the features distorted as in a fairground mirror, the collages of cuttings from the *National Enquirer*, the little Madonnas Kurt stole from the cemetery and on whose cheeks he painted blood tears, the kitschy figurines, the glass snowstorm spheres on which he drew giant cockroaches, the dolls that had been cooked in clay, headless dolls, dolls missing one eye or with a tortured limb, the transparent plastic anatomical models whose vital organs had been painted an unnatural color or put in the wrong position, the adulterated religious pictures, the dead insects caught by the fly-strips, the fishbowl where Kurt arranged his dioramas representing gruesome nativity scenes peopled by skeletons and decaying corpses, the fridge door decorated with photographs of diseased vaginas taken from a medical textbook that Kurt had stolen from a gynecologist.

When he went around to collect his weekly bag of system, Homer would always find him engrossed in his own little world of disquieting wonders. If he wasn't playing guitar, he'd be cutting out a photograph or putting a doll in the oven or recording commercials which he would later mix with political speeches or Christmas carols. He rarely went out and had a limited social life – not quite as limited as Homer's but not much better. He liked to stay at home and concentrate on his art. In one sense, given the kind of life he led, he might as well not have moved to Olympia, but he was still very glad he'd done it, glad to know that the town he'd gone to live in wasn't a community of redneck loggers like the one he'd grown up in.

Sometimes Tracy would get exasperated. 'Wherever I turn I find a mutilated doll staring at me,' she complained.

'Do you want me to leave?' asked Kurt impassively.

Tracy said nothing, because in a way she was trying to test his love for her. She often told him she loved him heart and soul, but he'd just say she shouldn't love him so much.

'If you want me to leave, you only have to say.'

'Where would you go?'

'I'd live in the car.'

'Don't be stupid.'

'I'm not being stupid. I've done it before and I can do it again.'

Kurt wouldn't have had much choice, to tell the truth. It was Tracy who earned the cash, who provided everything. She had a job and he didn't. She left for work at ten in the evening and didn't get home till morning. She did the graveyard shift in the Boeing cafeteria in Seattle. When she came home, he was asleep. When he woke up, she was in bed. They communicated via notes stuck to the fridge. Mostly 'to do' messages from her.

Kurt, she would write to him, please, before you turn on the TV, take out the garbage, empty the cat litter, put the dirty dishes in the sink, shake the mat, vacuum the front room, but before you do that sweep the dust out of the corners. Please, do that for me. Please, please, please. If I get back early we'll have a beer, then we'll fuck. Love you, Tracy.

When Kurt got up, around midday, he would read the memo and fill his conscience with good intentions. She's right, he would say to himself. But he always ended up procrastinating, and the first thing he would do was exactly what Tracy had begged him not to do: turn on the TV. Then he would fix himself something to eat, usually Kraft Macaroni & Cheese. When he'd finished eating he would leave his plate on the table and flop on the couch to watch TV for a couple hours. Then he'd practice his guitar, still watching TV. He'd spend about four hours like that, after which he would start messing around with his collages and his mutilated dolls, still with his eyes fixed on the TV. In fact it would be fair to say that he spent the whole day watching TV. Pretty much like Homer, in fact.

He lived like that for four years, in his protective, odor-filled shell, like a hermit in his cave. On the rare occasions when he went out it was to rehearse with the band or to play a gig somewhere. He had a band of his own now, a three-piece. There was him on vocals and guitar, and a strange guy on bass called Krist, who was so tall it gave you a crick in the neck to look him in the eyes. The third member was a constant variable in the form of drummers who were replaced at fairly regular intervals.

'What was the band called?' asked the talk-show hostess, who during the commercial break had done a meditation exercise to calm her nerves.

'They went through several names before they found the right one. Do you want me to tell you all of them?'

'Just the right one will do, thank you.'

'That's the only one I can't remember, I'm afraid.'

The hostess raised her eyes heavenward.

'But I can tell you it was one of those mystificatory words.'

'Mysti*what* words?'

'Buddhism and that kind of crap. You know the kind of thing, right?'

'Yes, yes, I know.'

'Well, this word I can't remember comes from the Sanskrit and means "extinction". Cool, huh?'

'Amazing.'

'Do you know where Kurt found it?'

'How in heaven's name *could* I know?'

'In Webster's. Isn't that amazing? He found it browsing through Webster's. It's incredible the words you can find in a dictionary, isn't it?'

'Truly incredible.'

'"The extinction of desire, passion, illusion and the empirical self. The attainment of rest, truth and unchanging being. The state of omniscient passive peace attained by a soul liberated from matter,"' Homer recited from memory.

The hostess was at a loss for words.

'It's like being in a place where nothing happens but you feel good anyway. The system's a bit like that, too. You know what it's like when you systemize yourself, don't you?'

'No, I do *not* know. What do you take me for, a junkie?'

Homer raised his eyebrows in surprise. He couldn't see what that had to do with the system.

'Are you trying to tell me something, Mr Alienson?' the hostess asked him, as icy as the pole star.

'I-I'm not sure I understand,' stammered Homer.

'No?' The hostess seemed suddenly more at ease. Much more at ease.

'I-I was referring to the system, not to dr...' The word wouldn't come out of his mouth.

'Drugs. You were about to say drugs, weren't you?'

'Being integrated into the system isn't like being a drug addict,' Homer protested.

'No?'

'No, absolutely not. It's not the same thing at all.'

'Well then, Mr Alienson, would you be so kind as to explain to the viewers at home what you take to be the meaning of the term "addiction"?'

Homer began to feel breathless.

'Well, Mr Alienson?'

For some reason, Homer was seized by an intense agitation bordering on panic. He felt stifled and he kept shivering, even though he was warm. He kept touching his face and rubbing his nose and cheek-bones with his fingers, and now and then with the whole palm of his hand. He tried to restrain himself, vaguely aware of how unpleasant it must look to the viewers at home, but he couldn't.

'We appear to have another of your memory lapses,' remarked the hostess with feigned regret. 'Let's see if our producer can help you.'

The studio lights dimmed, and on the luminous screen that formed a backdrop there appeared an enlarged, six- by nine-foot photograph of a dictionary definition of the word 'addiction'.

addiction n.\ ə'dicksh n, a'- [¹*addict* + *-ion*] **1**: *obs* : INCLI-
NATION, BENT **2a** : the quality or state of being
addicted; *specif* : the compulsive uncontrolled use of
habit-forming drugs beyond the period of medical need
or under conditions harmful to society <the extent of ~
ranged from 2 months to 10 years> **b** : enthusiastic
devotion, strong inclination, or frequent indulgence
<his ~ to the comics> <his ~ to frequent metaphors>.

137

'Would you mind reading out the text on the screen
behind us, Mr Alienson?'

Homer waved his hand to indicate that he would
rather not. His lungs had become as hard as titanium
and as heavy as lead; he couldn't breathe and felt as if
he was dying.

'Is anything wrong, Mr Alienson?' asked the hostess,
beaming with pleasure at Homer's discomfort. 'Shall I
read it for you?'

Homer tried to say something but only succeeded in
emitting a kind of hiss. As the hostess read out the definition of the word 'addiction', a studio technician
brandished in front of Homer an intimidating card
saying, in fluorescent orange marker, DON'T RUB YOUR
FACE WHEN YOU'RE ON SCREEN. Homer nodded to the

technician but continued to rub his face with the palm of his hand so hard it seemed as if he was trying to rip the skin off. The technician bared his teeth.

'Well?' said the hostess, when she had finished reading. She turned toward Homer, who stared back at her, open-mouthed with astonishment. 'Do you deny that you are addicted to what you call the system?'

'I am not a drug addict,' Homer managed to say with a surge of pride, summoning what little strength he had left. His respiratory crisis seemed to have subsided, at least for the moment.

'Really?'

Homer nodded wearily.

'But is it not true, Mr Alienson, that for the past three years you have taken heroin or, if you will, integrated into the system, on an almost daily basis?' she persisted, pretending to check what he had said in her large notepad covered with highlighted phrases, asterisks, exclamation marks and arrows connecting distant words by means of sinuous parabolas. 'And is it not also true that these *integrations* into the system are not isolated events, but are repeated several times in the course of a single day?'

Homer made as if to open his mouth but the hostess didn't give him a chance to speak. She was standing in front of him now. She stared down at him for a few moments, then leaned forward, gripped the arms of the swivel chair, brought her face to within six inches of Homer's, and looked him straight in the eyes. 'And is it not also true,' continued the hostess with a slower, more rhythmic cadence, 'that the frequency of your integrations into the system has been steadily increasing?' Homer had cowered as far back as he could in the swivel chair and lowered his gaze. The hostess, still looming over him, tilted her head to one side, waiting for an answer. In that position the jacket of her attorney-style suit ballooned forward, giving Homer full view of a distinctly icy bosom. He wondered if the producer had zoomed in to offer the people watching at home a furtive glimpse of that accidental décolletage.

'Mr Alienson?'

Homer felt cold now, freezing cold. He was squeezed back so hard against the back of his seat that he felt like his body had fused with the chair.

'I only wanted to sleep,' he moaned.

She tilted her head to the other side, as if she needed to view Homer from a different angle to assess his words correctly. She didn't really need to assess anything, of course. She was merely preparing the ground for her next rhetorical question. Homer was shaking like a leaf and his swivel chair squeaked plaintively, highlighting the drama of the situation. The soundman twiddled a knob to amplify the sound and the producer gave him an approving okay sign. The hostess stood there with her hands on the arms of the swivel chair, glaring at Homer, her bosom bulging forward in her jacket and rustling against the silk of the lining. Something had stirred in his stomach and now he felt it rise into his throat, accompanied by the acrid taste of gastric juices. He tried to swallow, but before he could do or even think of doing anything else, he realized that he had swamped the hostess and her suit with a foul, greenish liquid.

'He – he's barfed on me,' she yelped, retreating slowly from the swivel chair, like a toy robot whose batteries are running down. 'The fucking junkie's barfed on me.'

The studio assistant turned helplessly toward the producer. Another headset-wearing assistant was waving his arms about frantically like an aircraft-carrier signaler guiding in the planes. Homer had recovered somewhat and tried to banish the whole situation from his mind, vaguely aware that it was only imaginary, but it remained as painfully vivid as ever. The make-up girl had gone over to the talk-show hostess with a box of paper tissues and was trying to clean her up. The hostess, for her part, was standing so still, she might have been a photograph. Only her lips quivered, faintly.

'You fucking junkie asshole,' said the quivering lips.

Homer noticed that a fragment of undigested fried potato had gotten tangled in the hostess's vomit-soaked hair and for a moment wondered if he should draw this to her attention. In the meantime, however, a team of officers from the Drug Enforcement Administration had burst into the studio and surrounded Homer's swivel chair. Two of them grabbed Homer under the arms and physically lifted him out of it.

'Kick his ass. Beat the crap out of him,' screamed the hostess, while the make-up girl, having spotted the fragment of fried potato as well as a number of other assorted pieces of gunk, picked them off with a pair of nail tweezers which she periodically wiped on a tissue that she had spread out on her forearm.

Homer felt himself being dragged out of the studio and slammed against the plasterless wall of a dimly lit corridor. The officer in charge of operations addressed him in an affectedly amiable tone, while his two subordinates held him fast by the arms.

'Now, I don't think I need to emphasize that my friends and I have no wish to harm a hair of your head – though we all agree that this would be a far better world if trash like you weren't allowed to walk the streets. But since, as they teach in high school, this is a free country, if you come clean and don't give us any crap and tell us who you got it from, then maybe, and I repeat *maybe*, we'll let you go and fuck yourself up in perfect freedom. If you don't cooperate, however, we're going to be reluctantly obliged to break every bone in your body into such tiny pieces that you won't even remember you once belonged to the higher species of vertebrate mammals. I'm not sure if I've made myself clear, Mr Alienson.'

Homer was about to reassure the officer as to his powers of self-expression, even though he wasn't entirely sure what he was being asked to come clean about. But he didn't get the chance to articulate this rather incoherent line of thinking, because before he could open his mouth the DEA officer landed a punch right in the middle of his chest. Homer felt his ribcage crack and splinters of rib drive into his lungs. All the breath went out of him, and while he was still wondering whether he was only on the point of dying or was already dead, the officer searched his pockets and triumphantly extracted what he had been expecting to find.

'Here it is,' he said, with childlike glee to the studio assistant, who in the meantime had approached the theater of operations to see what was going on.

'What is it?' asked the assistant.

'A baggie,' replied the officer, showing him the exhibit. It was a glassine pouch about one square inch in size. 'Oh yeah,' said the assistant. 'It's one of those little envelopes philatelists use. My cousin sells that kind of stuff.'

'You're right, they are very similar,' said the officer, gazing at the bag as if it was the first one he'd ever seen. Then he shook himself out of his reverie and said: 'But the stuff they sell in these ones is smack.'

The assistant looked deeply shocked. Then, after a pause, he peered forward. 'There's a kind of picture on the outside,' he said. 'It looks like a woman.'

'That's the trade mark,' explained the officer, looking at the picture. It was a stylized portrait of a woman with long black hair and sensual lips. She was staring keenly out of the picture, like a snake about to bite its victim.

'Looks like a silent movie star,' hazarded the studio assistant.

'You're dead right. It's Theda Bara,' said the DEA officer. 'The first vamp in movie history.'

'Ah,' said the studio assistant, ashamed of his ignorance.

'She was the prototype of the femme fatale and man-eater,' said the officer, visibly pleased to have the chance to flaunt his knowledge. 'She used to do a kind of belly-dance on stage, and she wore Arab-style clothes, cut away to show off her curves. Theda Bara was only her stage name, though. She was a Jew, the bitch.'

'Yeah, but. . .'

'But what does she have to do with the stuff that was in this baggie, you mean?'

'Yeah.'

'You've got to understand that all shit – the white and the brown – is sold under trade marks like this one. The dealers choose exotic and evocative names to make them stand out on the market. It works like this: first they invent a new trade mark, print it on the bags and fill them with grade-four heroin, pure shit, so the junkies will only want stuff with that particular trade mark. Then, little by little, they dilute the drug with quinine, corn flour, sugar or even worse crap like talcum powder until, after a few weeks, there's hardly a trace of heroin left in the mixture, only the faintest smell. Finally, when the junkies show signs of going off the product, they either relaunch it by reverting to the old doses or invent a new trade mark using almost pure heroin, which they gradually dilute, and so the cycle starts over.'

'Ingenious,' commented the studio assistant.

'These guys know what they're doing. They apply highly sophisticated business strategies. But this stuff's different.'

'It is?'

'The reason they chose the name Theda Bara is that it's an anagram of *Arab death. . .*'

'You mean it comes from an Arab country?'

'No, the Colombians make it.' Before proceeding with his explanation he gave Homer another punch so that he wouldn't feel neglected. 'Until a short while ago they only produced cocaine, but now they've decided to get in on the smack scene, because it's becoming more profitable. The problem is, they don't have much experience in the refining process yet. The drug that comes out of their laboratories is kind of unmalleable; if you try to dilute it in the usual way you destroy it – it becomes completely unusable. So the dealers are forced to put it on the market exactly as it reaches them. We're talking ninety per cent pure heroin here.'

'Jesus,' said the studio assistant.

'You can say that again. The white shit is going to come back in. It'll be the pot of the Nineties, I'm telling you.'

The assistant's face indicated that he wouldn't doubt it. 'But isn't it rather – how can I put it? – repellent for a trade mark?'

'Are you kidding? They love that sort of crap,' said the officer, with a meaningful glare at Homer. 'You mustn't think they're normal people like us, my friend. They're different, very different. They're paranoid, hate-filled, self-destructive perverts. A repellent trade mark is just the kind of thing they're after. Blind Alley, The End, Terminus, Hell, Poison, Last Baggie, Overdose, Lethal Option – stuff like that, names alluding to death. Any normal consumer would find them repellent. But these guys are different. They think they belong to a separate world; they know they're shooting shit but take a snobbish pride in their own self-destructiveness. They think it's heroic to be a junkie – ' He broke off, possibly worried that he might be making addiction sound too attractive.

The studio assistant said nothing. The officer jerked his head toward Homer.

'Laughing boy here evidently didn't know Theda Bara is ninety per cent heroin, and this is the result.'

'Is that why he vomited over our hostess?' asked the studio assistant. Homer made a grimace to indicate that he hadn't meant to; the officer landed him a right to the jaw.

'Technically he's suffering from an overdose. Breathing difficulties, low blood pressure, sudden drop in body temperature. If he'd shot into a vein, he'd have dropped dead.'

'But isn't that how they take it?'

'I told you, this stuff isn't like the heroin they used in the old days. It's cheaper, and far better quality. You can get high just by sniffing it. Not even the psychological deterrent of the fear of the needle is going to help us from here on in. Hard times are coming, my friend. You mark my words.'

The assistant looked suitably concerned.

'Now, let's come back to you, pal,' said the DEA officer, grabbing Homer by his flannel logger's shirt. His two subordinates had stepped back and were watching with folded arms.

'Let's not complicate our lives more than necessary, shall we? Why don't you just tell me who gave you this stuff?'

'A f-friend,' said Homer with a piteous wheeze. The officer rammed his right knee into Homer's stomach. Homer doubled up and opened his mouth and eyes like a silent movie actor miming astonishment.

'You know why I had to do that, don't you, Homer?'

Homer hastened to nod, in case he got the left knee too.

'Okay. Now let's try again, shall we? Who gave you the stuff that was in this baggie?' And to make sure Homer had got his meaning, he gave him the left knee. Homer doubled up again, and remained bent over for a few moments. Finally, with a great effort, he managed to look up at the officer. His mouth was open and he did his best to speak but only succeeded in emitting some faint, guttural sounds.

'What did you say?' said the officer, grabbing him by the shirt and giving him another shake, for good measure.

'Kurt.' Saying the name was like vomiting a second time. For a moment Homer felt ashamed at betraying his friend, his *only* friend. Then he remembered he was only imagining this whole crazy situation, so he couldn't be described as a rat in the true sense of the term. Besides, he'd had enough; he'd say anything, if only they'd let him lie down for a bit and stop asking him questions and busting his ass.

'Surname?' said the officer, poised to hit him again.

Tears came to Homer's eyes as he realized that he didn't *know* Kurt's surname. He looked beseechingly at the officer, but how could he explain that in all the years he'd known Kurt he'd never once thought of asking him what his surname was? If he'd known what it was, he wouldn't have wasted their time, he'd have come right out with it. It would be stupid not to, when an imaginary officer was beating the shit out of you. Even the officer would have to agree that it was stupid to get your ass whipped for imagining you weren't betraying a friend. While Homer was lost in these thoughts and the officer was pondering what other part of his anatomy to hit him with, the talk-show hostess joined them in the corridor.

'Leave him to me for a minute, officer,' she said. She had regained her composure, and was now wearing a black silk dressing gown embroidered with golden oriental motifs. Without really knowing how, Homer found himself kneeling at her feet, and was alarmed to see that she was wearing pointed snakeskin boots. His hair was tugged back and he saw, from below, the hostess's face saying to him: 'What was that you were telling me about turtles and how much it hurts them if you knock on the shell, Mr System?'

He didn't even try to apologize for vomiting on her. He knew it wouldn't be any use, and simply resigned himself to his fate. The DEA officer, for his part, was quite happy to let her give Homer a rousting. It was only fair, really, he thought – the least compensation she deserved for the humiliation she had suffered on live television, in front of millions of imaginary viewers.

'I only have one thing to say, Mr System,' said the hostess. 'I trust it won't hurt *your* shell too much if I give you a kick in the balls.' And with an elegantly turned snakeskin boot, she aimed a kick at precisely that point.

Only then did Homer, and with him the whole unpleasant imaginary situation, finally black out.

He woke up to find himself lying on the couch at home, aching all over and still breathless, as he had been in the imaginary TV show. He turned toward the coffee table and saw that it was covered with a large pool of vomit. There were splashes on the TV set, too, which was still on, and framed the icy face of the talk-show hostess who'd interviewed him, only now she was a newsreader. She was talking about a girl called Melissa, the heroine of Operation Desert Storm and the most celebrated prisoner of war in living memory. The picture cut to Grand Rapids, Michigan, Melissa's home town, a scene of yellow ribbons and placards saying WE LOVE YOU MELISSA.

'Preparations have begun for the most spectacular parade ever seen in Grand Rapids,' said the talk-show-hostess-turned-newsreader. 'The guests include the President, the Secretary of Defense and the Secretary of State,' she added.

Apparently the Pentagon had refused to make any statement on Melissa's mental and physical condition, but a fleeting appearance by the girl in front of the television cameras had been enough to reassure the public. She was the picture of health and vitality in that yellow sweatsuit, with her hair gathered back in a ponytail and a wonderfully infectious smile.

CNN's Baghdad correspondent was interviewing her. Did Melissa know she'd appeared on the covers of countless magazines? Did she know she was as famous as a movie star? he asked.

'Wow,' Melissa had said, with a flash of that radiant smile.

Homer found the task of getting to his feet harder than he had ever done before. He couldn't understand the reason for all that pain, the breathlessness, the shivering fits, the stabbing pains in his abdomen. He felt unaccountably guilty for being such a physical wreck when other people – twenty-year-old girls, at that – had fought in the desert and been taken prisoner by the Iraqis. If he stopped breathing altogether and collapsed dead on the couch in a pool of his own vomit, maybe it would be no more than he deserved. He was little more than a parasite, after all. What did he ever do to earn the right to live? He preyed on guys who were stupid enough to pay enormous sums of money for tin flying saucers; he wandered around the house all day, doing nothing in particular and just waiting for evening to fall, so that he could systemize himself with the television on, vegetating in front of pictures that grew increasingly distant and blurred with every passing hour, until his catatonic stupor finally lapsed into a deep sleep that lasted for ten hours and more.

And when he woke up, all he was capable of doing was drinking a cup of coffee. And even that was largely a question of habit, because it tasted so bitter, no matter how hot he drank it, that at the very first sip he'd grimace with disgust and wonder why he bothered.

Then he'd walk down the road and into the woods, to take a stroll under the trees, where the sun never penetrated. Homer thought a walk among the trees might be a good idea now; he thought about the beneficial effects of the cold air, and while he was thinking he realized that the talk-show-hostess-turned-newsreader had suddenly grown serious.

'But while the celebrations are about to begin in Grand Rapids, elsewhere, in a small town in New Jersey, not far from New York, the flags are flying at half mast and the ribbons are not yellow, but black,' she said. Maria Rossi, a young Italo-American pilot of CH-47 Chinook heavy-transport helicopters, had died in a crash the day after the cessation of hostilities. A few days earlier she had been interviewed by the ubiquitous CNN man, who had asked her if she was scared of dying.

'I have been scared, and I still am,' Maria Rossi had said. 'But I'm a soldier. We all know our lives are hanging by a thread.' Then they had shown shots of the windows of the small town in New Jersey displaying photographs of Maria Rossi with captions saying things like WE'LL NEVER FORGET YOU.

On a sudden impulse, Homer picked up a paper tissue and began cleaning the splashes of encrusted vomit off the TV screen. He did this out of respect for that unfortunate, heroic girl and her tragic death. He cleaned carefully, almost solemnly, as if to apologize for not being Maria Rossi, apologize for not becoming the citizen that the Nation had hoped he would become, for only having thought of defending himself and of his own need to sleep, for being a coward, and for never once daring to confront those who were different from him. Perhaps he was also apologizing for becoming a junkie. When he stood in front of the mirror in the bathroom, where he had gone to freshen up, Homer seemed to see in his own reflection the equation of the system. Homer was to x as x was to Homer's need for x, where x equalled a progressively lower systemization with respect to Homer's needs. He had never been much good at math, but he was sure that if he could have done the calculation, the answer would have been something very close to 'You'd do anything to stay integrated in the system.'

He was part of the system, he was physically joined to it; he was so thoroughly systemized that to ask him to quit integrating himself would have been like asking 'different' people – ordinary, respectable people – to quit breathing.

But you systemize yourself with heroin, for fuck's sake. You can't seriously be comparing heroin to the air we breathe, said the respectable people. Homer pretended not to hear and put his hand under the faucet.

He withdrew it at once, because although the water wasn't cold, contact with it sent a shiver up his spine. He abandoned the idea of washing and went back to the couch. He felt a bit better now, though still short of breath. Pondering the shock the water had given him, he tried to remember when he'd last had a shower, but couldn't. He wondered how long he'd been wearing his flannel shirt. He couldn't remember that either, though to judge from the texture of the cloth it must have been over a month. He tried to recall what he'd done during the past month, apart from the usual things. He couldn't think of anything in particular. The electricity had been cut off because he hadn't paid the bill. It wasn't that he'd forgotten; he just hadn't done it. There was no real reason why he didn't pay those damn bills, except that he never actually did anything. If he ran his finger across any piece of furniture in the house, he'd collect inch-thick dust. Whenever he picked anything up, a spoon, say, or a pen, he'd put it down again wherever he happened to be when he felt the urge to do so. The spatial distribution of objects was an independent entity, entirely out of his control. Finding a thing could take days on end, because there was no logical way of reconstructing where he might have put it the last time he'd picked it up. Though actually none of his searches went on that long. Usually he'd look around for ten minutes or so, then think, fuck whatever it was he was looking for, he didn't really need it anyway.

He just didn't care about anything. Not that he had grown indifferent; the fact was, indifference personified was taking over the universe. Before long, not even God would give a damn about the world he'd created. The only exempt space was the coffee table. That was the only area that Homer looked after. He'd wipe it with his shirt cuff a couple of times a day. Then he'd scrutinize the surface to see if there were any traces of system left, moisten his finger with saliva and pick up the scattered grains, putting them in his mouth to savor the taste of heroin, which, though bitter, was not as revolting as the coffee he made. He also looked after the library card that he used to crush the powdered system, and the straw through which he inhaled it; they were the only objects that hadn't yet gained their independence from Homer. Well, there were the baggies, too. But they came and went. They were the system, what kept him going. They were a different matter.

It's not quite true to say that he never did anything.

He did a lot of looking. Or rather, he sat in absolute contemplation. If his gaze fell on any particular object – one of his shirt buttons, for instance – he would, provided he was sufficiently systemized, spend hours just staring at it. This was a pure, absolute activity which nothing could disturb. No thought could have made him forget the button; no other object crossing his field of vision could have caught his eye, for, beyond the immediate vicinity of the button, the world became one big gray screen on which there was nothing interesting to look at, nothing truly worth thinking about.

Admittedly, he didn't do anything else apart from that. He'd even grown lax about his space-toy business. He didn't reply to his customers as promptly as he used to; he allowed the letters to pile up, and weeks would go by without his bothering to go to the post office to check his mailbox. He couldn't care less about the nostalgia geeks, about the anxiety with which they waited for an answer, for confirmation of whether he had that particular Masudaya space capsule or not, and, if he had, what price he could quote them and when he would be able to send it. He didn't care if they only lived for their world of painted tin and plastic, just as he only lived for his white dust with its white light and white heat. He didn't give a fuck. The only times he remembered them were when he was short of cash; then he'd pick a couple of letters from the pile at random, write that, yes, he did have that damn capsule and that, sure, he would send it as soon as possible, but that first they'd have to send a check for a cool three hundred bucks because that toy was a real collector's item. Then he'd forget all about them again for a week or two.

Well, not exactly forget. He'd just stop thinking about them. Like he stopped thinking about the bills. Like he stopped thinking about anything else, except her – for now he had given her a sexual identity: she was not just 'the system' anymore, but heroine. She was the sole object of his thoughts.

But now and then these thoughts would be interrupted by recurrences of the question that had appeared in the early Nineties, shortly after Laura Palmer's body was found wrapped in a plastic sheet, shortly before Homer passed the halfway mark in the life he might have lived, if only it had conformed to the average expectancy for a male human being in those years of unease. Whenever the question appeared, it threw his life into turmoil, and it would continue to do so until Homer decided to get away, to set out on a journey of exploration through a world he'd never seen, heading for a place he'd never dreamed he'd see.

What about love?

4.

Home Run

Of the various theories that have been propounded recently one of the most widely accredited is that the question of love that disrupted the peaceful course of Homer B. Alienson's existence in the early Nineties was not in fact a question but a cloud. Although one crucial point has yet to be explained, namely how a love-shaped cloud can be distinguished from the large number of more common clouds shaped like things, people or animals, and from the even larger number of clouds that have no particular shape, this theory has found some support in the fact that at around that time, in the skies of the more northerly latitudes, sightings began to be recorded of a strange new type of cloud, the so-called noctilucent or firefly cloud.

The firefly cloud was a nocturnal, or, to be more precise, an evening phenomenon, a product of those moments charged with meaning and emotion that immediately follow sunset, when the mantle of darkness begins to cover our planet. It was a spectral apparition, a white form with a fuzzy outline which emanated an unnatural glow, like a ghost.

Apparently these clouds had been observed periodically in earlier times, but had always been such fleeting and occasional apparitions as to fall within the category of rare, unnatural phenomena. It was only toward the end of the second millennium that they began to appear with some regularity in the icy skies of the North, owing to the gradual intensification of a range of human activities, notably the destruction of the forests. The billions of termites that swarmed where large numbers of trees had recently been felled gave off a natural gas called methane, which rose up to join the methane emitted by coal mines, dumps and other sources of pollution. All this methane carried an increased amount of water vapor into the upper layers of the atmosphere, where it formed firefly clouds, which continued to be struck by the rays of the sun even after sunset, thus proving that in technologically advanced civilizations certain natural boundaries, such as that separating night and day, are destroyed in exactly the same way as the forests are, or at least blurred and confused into a single gray mass in which light and darkness are ever present but always dulled, suffused in a hybrid persistence, never truly light nor truly darkness.

Only a few days before the question of love first appeared, Homer took a trip to Olympia. He went around to Kurt's house but found only Tracy there. Kurt was out on some business connected with the band, but she said why didn't he wait for him, he should be back any moment.

163

The prospect of being alone with Tracy didn't appeal to Homer one little bit. He disliked being alone with anyone, apart from Kurt. What's more, he had a hunch that Tracy intended to take the opportunity to discuss her relationship problems.

He was right, though she approached the subject by a very roundabout route. Kurt seemed to be getting weirder every day, she said, and asked Homer his opinion.

Predictably Homer didn't have an opinion, so Tracy picked up Kurt's diary and said: 'Read that. If that isn't weird, I don't know what is.'

Homer didn't feel he could read anything as

personal as someone else's diary. Tracy told him he needn't worry, it was for Kurt's own good; but if he really didn't want to, she'd read it to him.

'"I'm a male age 23,"' read Tracy, '"and I haven't masturbated in months. I've lost my imagination. When I close my eyes, all I see is my father and TV news commentators. At best the occasional little girl. No voluptuous naked sex kittens. No pouty lips or bodies wincing in ecstasy. Nothing like that. Nothing."' She looked up at Homer and asked: 'Isn't that crazy?'

Why she thought it was crazy to write such things he couldn't imagine.

Shit, he thought. Why hadn't he said he'd come back later? He'd only dropped in to say hi and, while he was about it, stock up on a bit of system. But instead he'd let himself be buttonholed by this girl who was just looking for someone to pour out her troubles to. What did he care about her emotional problems?

'I'm really worried about his mental state,' added Tracy.

Homer's impression, however, was that she wasn't worried at all. Or rather that *that* wasn't what she was really worried about. The truth was, the band was going places. Kurt was busy every day now, and even earning a few dollars of his own. She was jealous, that was the real problem. Jealous of the band. She felt destiny was leading Kurt toward a world in which there was going to be less and less space for her.

'He has nightmares every night. He wakes up suddenly with tears in his eyes shouting that somebody's trying to kill him. He dreams about vampires and stuff.'

Homer wondered how Tracy could possibly know this when she worked nights at Boeing.

'And that's not all.'

Homer raised his eyebrows, without really knowing why.

'Then there's the way he behaves at gigs. Before he goes on stage, he daubs red blotches all over his arms and shirtsleeves, to make it look as if he was mainlining. Why would he want people to think he's a junkie?'

Homer kept quiet, hoping she would stop telling him all these things. But she didn't care whether he said anything or not. She rattled on and on until Kurt came home.

'She's been talking to you about us, hasn't she?' Kurt asked him.

Homer shook his head. Tracy had slipped away into the kitchen.

'Sure she has. She's never satisfied. If she had her way we'd be fucking all the time. She says it's essential in a relationship. I just can't do it. I don't have all that emotional intensity.'

Homer thanked heaven he didn't have such problems. Being on your own has its advantages, he thought. Love, he thought, and left the thought unfinished.

Kurt kept saying that maybe they ought to loosen up the relationship. Maybe it would be better to live apart for a while. Maybe they shouldn't live together anymore. Maybe they could go on being together but live apart. His talk was full of maybes but Homer knew that Kurt only said maybe because he would never have the strength to tell Tracy they ought to split up. He never had the courage to say things that were hard to say and probably he'd contrive to make her hate him, so that she'd say what had to be said without too many maybes.

That evening a friend of Kurt's called Damon dropped in. He had rented a video of *Straight to Hell*. They had something to eat and watched it. It featured Joe Strummer and Elvis Costello. It was a pretty lousy piece of film and had been panned by the critics, but all at once Damon pointed his finger at the screen and said: 'Hey, there's that girl who plays in that band from Portland.'

Kurt seemed rather interested but said nothing. Tracy sulked all evening. Damon fell asleep soon afterward and Homer had a kind of presentiment.

The girl in the footage had a very unusual name. Her name was Love.

Spring 1990. That was when the question first appeared. The event coincided with the announcement of the discovery of Laura Palmer's body on April 8th 1990, the day the pilot footage of the secrets of Twin Peaks was shown. Perhaps the coincidence was a trivial one, but that year there were many such curious clashes. The economic indicators, for example, showed clear signs of recession, thus conspiring against the wellbeing of the Nation.

At first Homer tried to pretend he hadn't heard, because he wanted to stay in his world of predictable things and regularly spaced-out moments. He didn't want the hands of time to start spinning round out of control again; he wanted everything to stay calm, inside the cushioned stillness of the system.

'What about love?' the question asked. Homer impassively went on doing the little or nothing that he did, as if nobody had asked him anything. But the question wouldn't be shaken off; it kept asking him ever more insistently: 'What about love?'

Sometimes he thought of replying that he was too busy defending his right to sleep, and that he couldn't run the risk of getting involved with a 'different' person – some body snatcher with the face of a pretty girl. But he rejected this idea. What right are you talking about? the question would have retorted, and he would have had no answer. When a guy thinks of nothing but himself, nothing but staying cocooned within his system of life, what rights can he claim to have?

These were the first signs of what was to happen later in the imaginary TV show, but Homer, of course, had no way of knowing that. What he did understand was that the question wasn't going to just disappear as suddenly as it had arrived; but still, for many weeks he went on doing the same things that he had always done, putting off the solution of the problem to some future time when he might feel better. For he was beginning to show some strange symptoms of malaise. At first they were only mild – vague feelings of weariness, dizzy turns, attacks of nausea, a slight cough. He might have dismissed them as perfectly normal ailments that were no cause for concern, had it not been for their chronic persistence. They never let up. Every day, at about the same time, the condition would appear in the form of minor complaints which with the passing of time grew slowly but inexorably less minor. Reluctantly Homer was forced to accept that it was somehow connected with the system. For only the system gave him a little relief, removing this discomfort that engaged him, body and mind – because it, too, became a thought, and one that tormented him even more than his physical disorders.

He took to systemizing himself in the daytime, as well, but not in order to sleep. Now he did it to avoid feeling sick. If he didn't systemize himself he felt bad, and the less he systemized himself the worse he felt. Something had stopped working like it used to, and Homer would have given anything to have things go back to the way they had been before, to the good old days when systemizing himself had been wonderful and it had seemed that nothing would ever change. But the trouble was that whenever he tried to focus on the good old days, he found that his sickness, in some inexplicable way, had infected the past too. If he thought back weeks, months, even years, it seemed to have always been hovering in the background, always been present in some manner that had eluded his perception. Concealed in the depths of his body, it had grown gradually, noiselessly, unobserved, till it was firmly rooted; and only then had it come out into the light. Sometimes Homer suspected that it might have established itself inside him the first time he'd systemized himself, but he suppressed this idea firmly, because the mirage of the good old days was all he had left. If he'd had to relinquish even the memory of that golden age he didn't know how he could have gone on.

The system was losing its old power. Homer yearned for the wellbeing he'd felt in the early days. Often he would stuff himself to the eyeballs with system, in the hope that more massive doses might bring back the old glories. When he had got beyond a certain stage – and it wasn't long before that happened – heroine could no longer do anything for Homer. Now it was him who must do something for her; he depended on her, he implored her not to make him feel sick.

Time as he had come to know it ceased to have any meaning. He wished it would go backward, but since he didn't know how to make it do so, he erased any idea of the future from his mind. For he sensed that tomorrow he would feel worse than today, and since today he already felt terrible, and yesterday hadn't been too great either, the distant past of the early days, when heroine had not yet dwindled to the status of a momentary respite in the unremitting discomfort, seemed the only thing he could fall back on. The fact that that past would never return was by no means a deterrent; rather, it intensified the awfulness of the present and his hope that the future would stop continuing to arrive.

After the chastening experience of the imaginary television interview, Homer began to admit to himself that he was *almost* a drug addict. In reality there is no difference between *almost* being an addict and *being* one – nor could there be, for you only have to take the tiniest dose of heroin every day to addict your body completely. But Homer claimed to see a difference, pointing to the indisputable fact that a junkie takes drugs for the sake of taking drugs, whereas an *almost* junkie takes drugs for reasons extraneous to the drugs themselves.

Did Homer wish to take drugs? No, he did not. He merely needed to sleep. Would you deny a poor human being his sacred right to sleep?

Later, sickness had come, and Homer had had to resort to heroine to keep it at bay. That, too, was surely justifiable. Why should he have to feel worse and worse, when a small dose of heroine could at least alleviate his sufferings?

One day Kurt took pen and paper and wrote him a letter.

'Dear Boddah,' the letter runs, 'it's one of those dreary Sunday afternoons when it does nothing but rain and as usual I don't have much to do, so I thought I'd write someone a letter. To tell the truth, every day's like this. Interminable and rainy. That's why I've been doing so much writing lately. It's better than nothing. When I'm not writing letters I usually write songs. But I couldn't face it today. So, you want to hear my news? Here it is. A couple of months ago I turned twenty-three. Twenty-three. I can hardly pronounce the fucking word. Twenty-three.'

Here the letter breaks off.

Kurt never finished writing it and never sent it.

Countless times Homer knelt before his heroine, begging her to make things like they used to be. But even if she'd wanted to, how could she have restored to him the joys of the early days? Have you ever thought of asking a woman whom you no longer desire as passionately as you once did to make you have the same feelings you had when she first let you kiss her? 'Why, sure, honey. I'll make everything like it used to be, and when it's just the way you want it, I'll make sure it never changes again, okay?' Is that what she's supposed to say?

Nothing was going to go back to the way it used to be.

Ever.

Nothing.

Even when Homer systemized himself almost to the point of obliteration, that thought would not let him rest. Nothing was going to go back to the way it used to be. And yet when he opened his eyes of a morning his first thought was of systemizing himself, his first action was to systemize himself, and this other nagging thought made not the slightest difference.

He had begun to systemize himself out of desperation for a good night's sleep. These days, the first thing he did when he woke up was to systemize himself again. That was a bad sign.

Kurt came back to Aberdeen because he needed to talk to his sister Kim about something. Since he was in the neighborhood, he went around to see Boddah.

'You know something? While I was driving over here I realized how much I miss this landscape,' said Kurt, staring into space. 'While I was driving past the farms outside Satsop I thought to myself, I wonder what it would be like to live around here. I could buy myself a farm and play with the band whenever I liked. We could throw a lot of parties and invite people over and nobody would bother us.'

Homer frowned. Kurt wasn't the partying type.

'A nice big ranch. Like Neil Young's in California. What do you think, Boddah?'

Homer pondered. Satsop was the site of a disused nuclear power station, as far as he recalled. Besides, Kurt was always saying Grays Harbor County was a place to get away from, a shithole inhabited by drunken redneck loggers. Homer agreed. But the countryside was beautiful. You had to admit that. All that green set off by the pallor of the sky.

'Did you see some place you liked?' he asked.

'Yeah,' said Kurt.

'Good,' said Homer, reflecting that Kurt wasn't very well off.

They were walking through the woods. Now and then they stopped to scrape the moss off the bark of the trees. It was cold.

Kurt said: 'I was at Mom's house today.'

Homer zipped up his jacket.

'Every time I go back, there's always the same tension. You think you've shaken off those memories but you haven't. They're still lurking there somewhere, and as soon as you enter a room you feel that shiver of unease run up your spine. That total depression. The atmosphere of resentment, the air stinking of bitterness. Slammed doors. Hostile silences.'

He seemed to have forgotten his idea of buying a house at Satsop. It was as if he'd never mentioned it, never even thought it. Homer was used to this kind of behavior. He knew his friend's ways. In a sense he'd always known them, instinctively.

'You go into your room, you look around and you see the Iron Maiden poster, with ripped and hole-filled corners, the stained rug, the sticky brown blotch on the ceiling from all the joints and cigarettes you smoked. And you remember what a miserable fucking adolescence you had.'

When Kurt was seven his mother split from her husband, and that was the first betrayal he experienced, the first step on the road toward his wretched future. The second, soon afterward, was his father's remarrying. The third, the fourth, the fifth, etc., etc., were the ease with which his mother switched men, every one a bastard and many of them far younger than she was.

When Kurt was fifteen, his mother was thirty-five and still an attractive woman. Men tended to notice her and she made sure they did. Even Kurt's friends noticed her, especially as she sometimes bought them drinks. When it wasn't too cold she would sunbathe in a bikini in the back yard. There wasn't any sun in Aberdeen, but there was always someone to peek through the fence.

Before the divorce, Kurt was as happy as the day was long, as the saying goes. To him his parents were more than gods, they were proof that nothing could hurt him, they were the certainty that there would be a family outing on Saturday, that they would take him out to play, to have an ice cream or maybe even to visit Disneyland, as indeed they did on one occasion.

But when his father told him and his sister that he and Mom were going to live apart for a while, Kurt felt as if they'd lied to him because of something he'd done wrong, though he didn't know what. He began to mistrust them and adults in general – to feel scared, to hate, to answer back, to shut himself up in his world of anger and dark thoughts, and everybody wondered how such a sweet little boy had grown so obnoxious.

'Why did you go there?' asked Homer.

'I wanted to talk to Kim about something.'

Apparently his sister was having an affair with a certain Jennifer.

'It's not an affair,' Kim said, firmly but calmly. 'She's my girlfriend.'

'Jennifer?'

'Yeah.'

'Jennifer.'

'I'm gay, Kurt.'

He wasn't surprised. 'Mom's kind of flipped out about it.'

'I can't help that.'

'Pretend she doesn't know, you can at least do that.' It wasn't a real solution, but in their family that was the only way of solving problems – not talking about them.

They fell silent for a while. They were in a kiddies' playground. Kim was sitting on a swing. Kurt hung his head and gouged little holes in the ground with the toes of his shoes.

'I know you've tried pot,' said Kurt when it seemed that neither of them had anything else to say. 'You've probably done acid too,' he said again. 'Or cocaine.'

Kim didn't understand what this had to do with her being gay. 'I've never touched cocaine,' she said.

'Maybe not, but you will.'

'What the fuck is that supposed to mean?'

Kurt put his hands in his pockets and retracted his head into his shoulders like a turtle. He was looking downward and Kim leaned to one side to try to look him in the face, to get him to say what he was driving at.

'You will,' he repeated at length. 'But if you ever touch heroin,' he went on in a strange tone of voice, 'I'll kill you. If I hear you've been doing heroin, I swear I'll come running and I'll kill you.'

It was crazy talk, but Kim sensed that her brother meant it. She also sensed that it wasn't really her that he was talking to.

'Don't worry,' she said calmly. 'I could never stick a needle in my arm.'

Kurt nodded and sighed. Then he said: 'I've decided to quit.'

Kim didn't ask him what he had decided to quit. She didn't know her brother was a junkie, or at least she didn't consciously know it. She nodded too and said: 'Don't ever worry about me. I'm never touching that shit.'

There was another pause. Neither of them knew where to look.

Then Kim said: 'I'm glad you've decided to quit. That's great.' Her voice broke and the word 'great' was almost inaudible.

'Yeah,' said Kurt.

Kim's eyes had become moist and she kept turning away so that she wouldn't meet her brother's gaze, so that he wouldn't see that her lips were trembling.

The only sound was the blowing of the wind.

'Don't totally give up on men,' said Kurt, breaking the new silence that had fallen between them. 'I know they're assholes. I'd never date a guy from around here.'

Now it was Kim's turn to hang her head.

'I...' said Kurt but didn't finish the sentence.

'What?' said Kim, tears trickling down her cheeks.

Kurt grimaced and said: 'Nothing.'

Kim suddenly dropped from the swing and ran off.

Kurt watched the wooden seat sway back and forth in the dark and listened to the metallic groan of the chains grow gradually fainter.

Laura Palmer was found naked, wrapped in a transparent plastic sheet, her body mutilated by stab wounds. All that was left of her homecoming-queen beauty was the smile immortalized in the framed photograph that stood like a relic of domestic happiness on the mantel of the Palmer home.

How beautiful she was. She was so beautiful that *People* magazine included her in its list of the twenty most attractive people of the year. Who had dared to harm such a creature? America couldn't understand, America wanted to know. 'Who killed Laura Palmer?' people wondered, and to find out the answer they took to staying at home every Thursday evening, because it had become inconceivable to turn up at work on Friday morning if you weren't able to talk knowledgeably about what was happening in *Twin Peaks*. For many weeks, in many American homes, every Thursday there was a Laura party where people stuffed themselves with donuts, cherry pie and beer in front of the television. Homer, too, followed the course of the investigation, but he did so in solitude, stuffing himself with a very different substance.

Why deny it? He had a crush on Laura Palmer, just like everybody else, even though she no longer existed, even in TV fiction. She had become a regret even before she could pretend to be a real person, but maybe that was the secret of her charm. Regrets had a profound effect on Homer, for his life seemed to have become one great longing for the system that had been and that now was no more.

It was thanks to Laura Palmer, and to Homer's growing nostalgia, that the question of love succeeded in taking root. At the very time when Homer was beginning to see the system for the femme fatale that she was, he was fatally attracted to a woman who no longer existed.

Besides, the world of *Twin Peaks* in a sense was his world, the dismal Northwest world of damp, cloudy landscapes, of wet muddy roads traveled by log-laden trucks, of sawmills grinding out shrill metallic shrieks, of alcoholics walking around in plaid flannel shirts, of wannabe pompom girls who permed their hair in fancy ways to get screwed by some good-looking jock who would turn them into depressed or psychotic or downtrodden women. A life sunk in the gray desolation of the provinces where the houses exude the sinister smells of homemade cakes and cups of steaming black coffee, and the drapes at the windows hide the perverse, bloodthirsty intimacy of hopeless families. Kurt himself used to say that Aberdeen was like *Twin Peaks* without the mysteries – though whether the town really had no mysteries remained to be proven.

Then there were the trees. How could we forget them? Even FBI agent Dale Cooper, when he came to *Twin Peaks* to investigate Laura Palmer's death, was awestruck by them. 'I've never seen so many trees in my life,' were the first words he spoke on his arrival.

Strangely, Laura seemed to have something in common with Homer. In essence she was a wholesome country girl, a gentle, blonde-haired saint whose natural destiny was to remain pure until one day, as if by magic, she found herself a mother. She had tried to live up to that ideal, and she might have succeeded if it hadn't been for the insidiousness of the environment, the twisted minds of the people who dragged her down. Whenever she had tried to be good, something had pulled her back and she had plummeted downward, ever more firmly manacled to her nightmare. The effort of climbing back up to the sunlight that made her blonde hair gleam had grown harder, more impossible, every time. Homer, too, could have been different if it hadn't been for the hostile environment in which he was compelled to live. He, too, sank ever lower, despite his best endeavors.

But in other ways Laura was more like the Aberdeen differents. Like them, she had many secrets. Despite her innocent appearance, there was a dark core in her heart which gradually rose to the surface. As the episodes went by, she was revealed to be a psychologically disturbed, sexually promiscuous porno movie actress, who might well have ended up a whore, if she hadn't been murdered. She was also a drug addict, but even in this she was different from Homer, for she used cocaine, a very different drug from the system into which he was integrated.

As one Thursday evening followed another, the mystery of *Twin Peaks* deepened and many, including Homer himself, began to suspect that the answer to the initial question would be put off from episode to episode till it lost all importance. After a few months, the serial was teeming with freaks of every kind – seduced and molested girls, people who had gone out of their minds, people who had never had a mind, people who concealed secrets even darker than the name of Laura Palmer's murderer. The truly decent inhabitants of *Twin Peaks* could be counted on the fingers of one hand – and they had all paid a high price for their goodness. Donna Hayward's mother, for example, was confined to a wheelchair.

Perhaps evil wasn't a human quality at all, but something you breathed in the air. Malignant presences merged with the mist and perhaps lurked in the woods. Homer did have his doubts about the trees, but he loved them and was sure they were harmless. Then he thought of the owls and their lugubrious hoots in the night. The people of Grays Harbor County hated owls. Many a car drove by with an I HATE OWLS sticker on its rear window or next to its license plate. This antipathy had a basis in fact. Owls were an endangered species in the area, so a law had been passed limiting the number of trees that could be felled, and this had precipitated the final collapse of the precarious timber economy.

The owls needed the woods for survival and refuge. Homer read in an encyclopedic dictionary that they were birds of ill omen. He read that the owl was sacred to Athena, the Greek goddess of wisdom, that Athena was created out of the mind of Zeus, and that she represented the male view of the world. This last point puzzled Homer. How could a goddess represent the male view of the world? he wondered. Was Athena really male? Perhaps even the owls were not what they seemed.

The boundary between good and evil became increasingly blurred. Perhaps good was only an ingratiating smile on the face of evil. He could no longer tell the difference between the innocent Laura portrayed in the photograph on the mantel and the promiscuous corpse-Laura whose lips were tinged with the icy blue of the ominous dawns of Washington State. The grounds of comparison were crumbling beneath his feet. What did it matter whether a woman was a virgin or a whore, when it was the nature of woman *per se* that had brought the whole town low?

Laura Palmer, the imaginary talk-show hostess, Theda Bara, Heroine, Becky Driscoll. . . he worked his way back up the list of the women in his life till he reached his mother. He remembered the way his mother got men to look at her and the time he'd told that cop about it. It was all too much for him. The world was just too different. They were all in it together, except him. Even heroine seemed to have dug an underground tunnel that she could crawl along to meet the differents and make a deal with them. He was truly alone; for the first time in his life he felt the need for a woman. The question was right. It was right to keep on asking him.

What about love?

'Yeah, you're right. Love. . .' he answered dejectedly, and burst into tears. The TV was showing film of a twenty-three-year-old girl who was dying because she'd caught the new immune-deficiency virus from her dentist.

* * *

On one of the many days when he never left the house, Kurt wrote a letter to somebody.

'Listen, you guys, my non-existent friends,' said the letter, 'you're the only people I can talk to or fool around with. Why don't we have a talk about books and how to change the world? Afterward, we could go out and have a good time. Huh? Wouldn't you like that? . . . I'm asking you PLEASE! Christ, I can't stand it any longer in here, banging my head against the wall. Please! Can't you give me a little affection? At least try. That's all I ask. I need some friends so bad. . . why don't you answer me? shit shit shit, isn't there anybody out there in that fucking world of yours? . . . somebody, anybody, anybody at all. . . I can't stand it anymore, sitting in here with only my dreams to comfort me. I'm so lonely. So. . . Is there anybody out there? Why don't you say something? Answer me, please. . .

please. . .'

While Homer B. Alienson was finally yielding to the question of love, America went to war and *Twin Peaks'* viewing figures tumbled. But CNN's around-the-clock coverage of events in the Gulf was only the culmination of a crisis that had begun with a scheduling change whereby *Twin Peaks* was switched from Thursday evening to Saturday evening. The move was a disaster, because the serial's audience was chiefly made up of youngsters, exactly the sort of people who could never be persuaded to stay at home on weekend evenings.

Even Homer had lost interest in the events surrounding Laura Palmer. Even he, the quintessential couch potato, a man who spent every evening at home with the TV on and who had never had the problem of going out on Saturday with friends, since he didn't *have* any friends. Apart from Kurt of course, but that was another matter. The fact was that the secrets of *Twin Peaks* had become too numerous even for someone like Homer, who merely watched the figures moving about and didn't worry too much about the story.

Homer, and everybody else, had tired of trying to keep up with the vagaries of producers who had turned a simple question like WHO KILLED LAURA PALMER? into a tangled web of implausible plots. They had turned a dreary Northwest town into a haven of specters, murderous spirits, flying elves and aliens. A thriller's a thriller, for God's sake. Rule number one in the *Detective-Story Writer's Rulebook*: supernatural beings and preternatural events are *out*. The investigator must arrive at the solution not through vague hunches or paranormal contacts, but logical analysis of the known facts. The odd exception, the occasional bit of fantasy, is acceptable, but a federal agent who is constantly muttering into a dictaphone as if he were whispering sweet nothings to his girlfriend was just too much for a cliffhanger serial. Not to mention a slew of other oddities so way out that you wouldn't have tolerated them even in *Star Trek*.

Not that the TV audience considered the matter so rationally. They simply got fed up. Even the revelation that Laura Palmer's murderer was none other than her father did nothing to revive the show's fortunes. When it was finally taken off the air only a handful of diehard fans were left to protest by sending the network threatening letters and boxes of moldy donuts.

Lonely Homer, for his part, did the most reasonable thing in the circumstances: pending the arrival of yet another new generation of *Star Trek* with characters even weirder than those of *Twin Peaks,* he bought a box-set of videos of the original series starring Captain Kirk and Mr Spock.

One day Kurt wrote him another letter.

'Dear Boddah,' the letter begins, 'I haven't slept a

wink all night. I don't know how to tell you this, but I've killed one of my rats. You know the ones I mean, the ones I keep in the house with the turtles.'

Homer knew the ones he meant.

'Kitty. I've killed Kitty,' the letter continues. 'I let him out of his cage, as I do sometimes. Anyway, there was this spider on the ceiling and I said to him, See that fucker, Kitty? Get him, kill him, the fucker. But he didn't, so I went into the bathroom and got the deodorant to spray it on the spider but when I went back into the room I heard a horrible noise under my foot. Christ, Boddah. I trod on Kitty's head. He jumped around the room squeaking and bleeding and I screamed, Forgive me, Kitty. I didn't mean to do it. I'm sorry, I'm sorry, I'm sorry. I said I'm sorry thirty times. Then I had to catch him and I put him in a plastic bag. I went outside and I crushed the bag with a piece of two-by-four. To put him out of his misery. I heard the scrunching of his bones.'

Homer heard it too and shuddered.

'I carried on for two minutes to put him out of his misery and then I went into misery for the rest of the night. When I went back indoors I saw the bloodstain on the floor and the spider still there on the ceiling. I screamed Fuck you! at him. I thought about killing him, but I didn't.'

When he had finished reading, Homer wondered why Kurt kept writing him letters and never sending them.

Homer had no wish to fly in the face of nature, nor was he against changes in principle. All he asked was that changes should treat objects with respect. His reasoning was as follows: when you pick up an object in order to use it, once you've finished using it you put it back; and when you borrow some money, after a while you give it back, right? Just think what a mess the world would be in if people never put things back or repaid their debts. Homer wondered why changes couldn't do the same; why they didn't put things back where they'd found them or return them to their owners after they'd had their fun with them.

What with his obsession with the differents and his refusal to sleep in case they changed things while he slept, Homer himself had become one of those nostalgia geeks that he so much despised. Only he didn't collect toys, but empty baggies. He'd systemize himself with heroin and then, when the heroin was finished, he'd take the empty baggie and put it somewhere – fix it on the fridge door with a turtle-shaped magnet, jam it under the frame of the bathroom mirror, or insert it between the pages of some book he'd particularly enjoyed reading. The house was littered with empty glassine bags. If a DEA agent had raided Homer's house it wouldn't have taken him long to find what he was looking for. This nostalgia of Homer's was all part of his obsession with reliving the golden age when he'd first systemized himself with heroin. It was this that had turned him into a collector of baggies marked White Shit, Mainline, Poison, The End, Stardust, Lethal Dose, and of course Theda Bara.

These baggies scattered around Homer's house were like the photographs of Laura Palmer that stood on so many mantels. They evoked memories of a harmonious system of life that had never really been harmonious, just as Laura's picture evoked memories of a nice girl who had perhaps never really been nice. They were relics of a personalized past, fetishes which evoked reassuring, or at least consoling, memories.

Homer wanted to be reassured that life is a cycle, made up of things that come, go and return. All he asked of those things that fell into the cursed category of things that do not return was that he should at least have the consolation of tangible proof that they had existed, that he hadn't imagined them. For Homer was no longer entirely sure that there had ever *been* a golden age of the heroin system. He'd gone half his life without sleeping, with daydreams instead of dreams. He was seeking the past without having a memory. For nostalgia and memory are not the same thing; indeed they have nothing at all in common. Nostalgia preserves the past of the things we like to remember, whereas memory preserves that of the things we wish we could forget.

One day Kurt's mother, too, wrote a letter. It was addressed to the many mothers and fathers who had sons like Kurt, but since it would have been crazy to send the same letter to so many people she sent it to the Aberdeen newspaper.

'All you parents whose children split your eardrums banging on drums or twanging on guitars, mind what you say to your children.' So began the letter. 'Mind what you say, because you might end up having to eat your parental lectures. Like, "Why don't you get yourself a career instead of playing guitar all day? Life is hard and music won't feed you." I've had to eat mine. Yesterday my son called me. He plays guitar and sings in a rock band. They've made a record and soon they're going on tour to Europe.

Kurt, if you read this letter, I want you to know that we're all so proud of you and that you're the most wonderful son a mother could ever hope to have. Now that you're away from home, mind what you eat, remember to clean your teeth and when you go on tour and sleep in a hotel mind the maid makes your bed properly. I love you, Kurt.'

'Being human does have certain advantages. For example, it enables you to appreciate the beauty of a flower or a woman,' said Captain James T. Kirk, the great intergalactic Lothario, on one occasion.

There was no denying that the commander of the starship *Enterprise*, on his five-year mission to explore new worlds and seek out new forms of life, put these advantages to good use, seeking out new, agreeably female forms of life, a succession of young women to be charmed, seduced, bewitched, conquered, sometimes even loved, but always ditched before the final credits.

In episode after episode, *Star Trek* offered a unique cross-section of all the beauties one might possibly meet, though Homer had his doubts that some of them really existed. No woman resembling Marta, the green-skinned Orion dancer, had ever been seen in Aberdeen, even in the days of the 'women's boardinghouses'. Nor had any like Kelinda, the icy Kelvan whom Kirk finds the time to seduce while the crew of his spaceship are immobilized in tetrahedral blocks.

Fascinated by the ease with which Captain James T. Kirk met these beautiful alien women, Homer made a 194 mental note of his romances in the hope of fathoming their secret, or at least taking them as a model, should he ever decide to answer the ever more insistent question of love. Though skeptical about the authenticity of the TV serial, he couldn't help believing in it. Or half-believing, anyway.

It's amazing how much bullshit people can get away with on TV, Homer often thought to himself. He wondered if any Trekkies had ever written complaining letters to the writers of the serial or to the director of the network that showed it. He knew what they were like, these fans of hypothetical, extraordinary, not-scientifically-attested events. He knew how their minds worked. They were like the nostalgia geeks, people with nothing better to think about. Fact fanatics. They loved their bullshit, but it had to be believable. Now hold on a minute, just because it's called science fiction, it doesn't mean you can fuck about with science: that was their attitude. They were the sort of people who would get all steamed up about the miscalculated length of an episode and yet happily put up with entire seasons of a serial featuring pointy-eared characters and starships that traveled at Warp Eight.

Yeah, those guys got on his nerves. He'd never met one in his life – God forbid he ever should – but he'd worked out what they were like. He'd only had to watch a few of those pieces of footage to understand that they were just like the collector geeks. Okay, it might be objected that he himself spent all his time watching the same kind of film, but that was different. For one thing, he would never have dreamed of watching such crap if he hadn't had the problems he did have. Secondly, he didn't watch footage and all the other stuff they showed on television for its own sake; he watched it because he systemized himself, because it was conducive to systemization and sleep. What was he supposed to do, for Christ's sake? Systemize himself with heroin and sit there staring at the coffee table? There was a practical usefulness in his TV-watching, that's patently obvious. Surely we don't need to argue about that, too.

* * *

'Yesterday wasn't a bad day, Boddah,' begins one of those letters that Kurt never sent. 'Would you believe it? I earned ten dollars for a painting.'

Homer agreed that this was hard to believe.

'Listen. This girl called Amy, who lives downstairs, knocked on the door, and I'd just finished painting a great picture. So I said to her, Take a look at this. I've done it with acrylics, as usual, with one special addition. My secret ingredient. The final touch – sperm. And I put the painting under the light to show her how it glistened. Amy looked at it and said nothing. She didn't dare ask me how I got it onto the canvas. But she wasn't grossed out. In fact, she commissioned me to depict a dream she'd had. She gave me ten dollars for the materials and described the scene. A nocturnal landscape with some trees, and in the foreground the headlamps of a car and a deer that had just been run over. She told me to paint the breath coming out of the deer because it was visible in the dream. And to show that the body was warm, if possible. And a very thin female figure eating the deer's flesh while it was still alive. I asked her if there was anything else and she said no, that was where the dream ended. So I said okay and painted it all exactly as she wanted. It turned out pretty good.'

* * *

He bought himself a special lamp. It was a British import called the Astrobaby, one of those lava lamps that were so fashionable in the Sixties. It consisted of a glass bottle containing some purple liquid and a block of wax. The bottle had to be slotted in between two chromium-plated metal clips that formed the base and the top, giving it a vaguely spaceship-like appearance. The actual lamp was concealed in the base and illuminated the purple contents from below, turning the bottle into a ghostly psychedelic fishbowl.

Once the lamp had warmed the bottom of the bottle, the block of wax started to melt and change shape. You saw it grow longer and thinner until a smaller block broke away from the main body like a soap bubble and rose slowly upward, undulating slowly in the purple liquid. There came a moment when the bubble ceased its slow ascent and lay still, suspended in the upper part of the psychedelic bottle. A couple of seconds at most, then the bubble sank back down toward the luminous base to reunite with the block from which it had broken away. For a moment you had the illusion that the block had settled down, exhausted by its own weight, but the heat of the lamp wouldn't let it rest; it heated it, making it stir again, and the cycle was repeated, the block grew longer and thinner again and new bubbles broke away in their short-lived attempt to reach a non-existent surface. Like fish that turn around when they come up against the transparent wall of a fishbowl, the bubbles wafted limply back down to fuse once more with the lavic mass, the pulsing heart that awaited them in the luminous depths of the bottle.

Homer had placed the lamp on top of the TV and spent countless hours gazing at the metamorphic contortions of the wax, forgetting all about the pictures flickering across the screen below. The Astrobaby's hypnotically slow dynamics reminded him of the sublime state of muffled undulation that the system used to give him in the good old days, a state that he now experienced only seldom and fleetingly. So he took to systemizing himself with heroin with the Astrobaby on, fishing for remnants of the golden age in the psychedelic depths of a lamp that illuminated nothing. For that mysterious, fascinating object also embodied a contradiction: it was not what it should have been. If you turned off all the other light sources, the room was plunged into darkness, because the Astrobaby's purple glow only lit the contents of the bottle. It was a strange phenomenon: the lamp shed light, but only on itself.

From a logical point of view this was quite a puzzle, because you couldn't say the Astrobaby wasn't a lamp, since it did light up, but you couldn't say it was one either, since it didn't give off any light. It was like a radiator that only heats its own pipes or a knife that only cuts its own blade. It was a true object for daydreamers, something you couldn't just take at face value.

After hours of catatonic contemplation, it dawned on Homer that the Astrobaby was not a lamp at all, but a psychedelic hourglass. The idea was the same: the lava went up and down like the sand in a normal hourglass; only this hourglass didn't need to be turned upside down, because the light's heat ensured that the wax kept moving. So as well as being psychedelic, it was perpetual. At least until the light bulb failed.

The more he gazed at the Astrobaby in his heroin-systemized state, the more convinced he became that it wasn't simply a lamp but a luminous time machine that worked in the same way as heroin did: exploiting light and heat to control the flow of time. There were only two differences. The first was that heroin was a different color from the lamp. The second was that you could ingest heroin, whereas apparently you couldn't drink the liquid of the Astrobaby. For on the bottle's cap there was a printed warning, 'Do not remove or drink contents'.

There is a letter of Kurt's which reads:

'People think life is so sacred. They think it's the only chance you get. So a lot of people think they must do something important in their lives, because they see life as something realistic. But I think it's just an intermediate stage, a sort of midterm, to test how you're coping with reality. I don't know what reality is, but I'd dearly love to ask the people who *do* know the reason for all the insecurities that have afflicted me these past twenty-three years. I'd like someone to explain to me clearly why I don't want to learn anything more from life. Yesterday I went shooting with Dylan in the woods. He's a gun fanatic. I've been going there with him for a while now. I never would have done it in the old days. I always thought it was stupid to play with guns, but finally I let Dylan explain to me how to take aim and pull the trigger and stuff. But we don't hurt anyone. We shoot at empty cans or I choose one of my paint-ings that I don't like anymore, we load it in the car, take it to the woods and blast it to smithereens. Don't ask me why I do it – I don't know. It's just that sometimes I feel like Hamlet, like I had to choose between life and death, between reality and a ghost that is not my stomach pain. I've even lost the ability to enjoy being sad.'

Sometimes Homer looked around and noticed the desolation of his house. Objects that had lain neglected in the most unexpected places for God knows how long, little curls of fluff that slid along the floor carried by mysterious air currents like the tumble-weeds that bounce on the Arizona desert, mantles of dust that coated everything, empty baggies like so many little flags planted on a newly discovered planet called Waste.

The glassine baggies reminded him of the wrappers in which the owners of the collectors' stores kept the old comics, those historical records of the deeds of the superheroes. He felt a dreadful affinity, in the desolate discomfort of his existence, with nostalgia geeks like Jim and their excruciatingly sad lives; his own life seemed to have been poisoned by the diseased waters of time that flowed in the River Nostalgia.

He remembered his first visit to one of those stores, in Olympia, and the shiver that had run down his spine, that mixture of cold and sweetness, like the touch of the lips of a dead girl climbing out of her plastic wrapper and creeping up behind him. He remembered the tinkling of the door as it opened and the ruffling of the sheets of paper on the noticeboard, those pathetic little rectangles stirred by the gust of cold air that blew momentarily into the store. That was when it had all started. Since then, Laura Palmer's body had lain abandoned in the great forests of the Northwest and in the darkness of unknown, hidden thoughts. That was long before David Lynch had found her, but she had seen Homer and had awoken for an instant from her eternal sleep to come over and kiss him on the neck.

Why had it happened? he wondered. And had it really happened? And how many years had passed since then? Heroin had swallowed up all that time, had so permeated everything that all the time that had gone before – the years of his sleeplessness – no longer seemed to belong to him. It was like a sad tale of someone else's life that he had ended up sharing out of compassion.

He thought about the background noise of all things, the echo of the great cosmic bang of creation whose residual wave spread throughout invisible matter, the missing mass of the universe carried by a wind that blew from the beginning of the world, a wind that those two radioastronomers had at first mistaken for interference caused by pigeons' droppings on their horn-shaped antenna. It had been the night he had met Kurt, the night when he had gone out in the absurd hope of capturing that impossible sound with the feeble human ear. He thought about the scream that he had heard someone hurl into the night, a scream so similar to the ones he himself hurled as he lay on the riverbank. He thought about the winds, the cold winds that kissed you on the neck and the supra-audible winds that blow throughout eternity. Maybe the question of love, too, was a wind, maybe Laura Palmer's cold lips which had brushed his neck in that store in Olympia had also whispered to him a question that he hadn't heard: 'What about love?' Or maybe that same question had traveled along, clinging to dark matter, had traveled light years, riding the residual wave of the cosmic bang, so that Laura's body might rise up from its plastic wrapper and whisper to Homer, 'What about love?'

Perhaps he'd been promised to a princess from some distant, forbidden planet, but didn't yet know it. Princess Heroine of the planet System – a girl as awesomely beautiful as space and as white as heroin, who loved him and would carry him away, far from uncertain futures, far from the differents, far from discomfort and from nostalgia for things he had never had and people he had never been. His love from another world.

204   He must get away from Aberdeen. What kind of love would he ever find in such a place? It was still the same hotbed of differents that had blighted his childhood. There was not a single person in the town he could relate to. He couldn't even establish a normal relationship with that devious clerk at the post office, let alone with such an intrinsically different and elusive creature as a woman.

Once he had tried. To start a relationship with an Aberdeen girl, that is. She worked at a supermarket checkout and smiled at Homer whenever he lined up to pay. Her smile was beautiful and her name, according to the identity tag pinned to her white coat, was Jackie.

One day he decided to wait for her outside the supermarket. He was feeling unusually optimistic at the time. Jackie had been smiling at him more warmly of late. When she smiled like that, it seemed anything was possible, even that a guy like Homer could go out with a girl like Jackie.

He took up position about twenty yards from the staff entrance and waited for her to emerge. He waited a long time – nearly three hours – by the end of which he was shivering, because the weather was bitterly cold. And when she finally appeared, his whole plan suddenly seemed crazy. He wished he'd stayed at home watching television, systemized up to the gills. He wondered what on earth had possessed him, what the hell he had thought he'd seen in what was after all only a smile.

She probably gave that same warm, confidential smile to all the supermarket's customers. She probably wasn't even called Jackie. The manager had probably told her to do those things, call herself Jackie and smile at the customers. He had been an idiot to fall for it. Thank God he had finally realized how things really stood.

But just as this realization was dawning on him, the girl came over and eyed him challengingly. For Homer, without being aware of it, had been staring at her all this time. He had been standing there staring at her as the truth sunk in, and now she was staring back at him. And this time she wasn't smiling. The expression on her face was rather ominous. It seemed to say, 'What the fuck are you staring at, you moron?'

Homer made a wry expression but said nothing, because he'd lost his voice. Then he took a sheet of paper from his inside pocket and offered it to her, his hand trembling pathetically.

'Is this for me?' she said.

He nodded. It was a drawing he had done in his high-school days and something had prompted him to give it to Jackie.

Jackie looked at it. It depicted a little green alien who had just disembarked from his spaceship. He was standing on a desert island scattered with palm trees and coconuts – the classic Robinson Crusoe setting, in other words. Homer had intended the little green man as a kind of self-portrait, a metaphorical representation of his sense of being an outsider. The island symbolized solitude, but also a far-off world where it was possible to start a new life. The drawing seemed to convey contrasting feelings: on the one hand the quest for a home, on the other a desire to escape. The alien's expression was suitably inscrutable.

The girl gave a forced smile. 'Thank you,' she said.

'Don't you like it?' asked Homer.

'Oh yeah, I like it very much,' she said, but it was clear she didn't. 'Did you do it?'

'Yeah, when I was in high school.'

'Oh,' she said. 'You were good at drawing.'

Homer changed the subject. 'Sometimes I come and shop in the supermarket where you work.'

'Sure.' The girl looked around.

'You can keep it, if you like.'

Jackie put the drawing in her pocketbook, looking around again. 'Thank you,' she said again.

Homer said nothing.

'Well, if there isn't anything else, I'll be going.'

Homer shrugged.

'Bye,' she said and moved slowly off, swaying her hips.

Homer nodded and put his hands in his jacket pockets. Jackie turned for a moment to look back and then walked on, quickening her pace. And that was all. Nothing else happened, except that now, whenever Jackie saw Homer line up at the checkout she called a colleague to take over from her.

'You should have told her you wanted to go out with her,' Kurt said when Homer recounted the episode to him.

'Would that have changed anything?'

'No, but she was expecting it. She probably thought you were a weirdo. Don't let that worry you, though.'

Homer did let it worry him a bit, if he was honest.

'It's always like that,' Kurt went on. 'There's always someone expecting something of you, expecting you to do something. They couldn't give a shit really, but they expect it. It's a kind of stupid fucking rule and it's one of the reasons why the world is crap.'

Kurt hated doing what people expected him to do, and made a point of doing the exact opposite. In his relations with the opposite sex, in particular, he'd always been contrary. He hadn't seen eye to eye, for example, with one of his mother's boyfriends, a guy she was dating when Kurt was sixteen. He was a womanizer; Kurt loathed him and was determined not to be like him when he grew up.

'Why don't you bring some girl home with you, instead of mooning around all day?' the guy would say to him every time he came over to see his mother. 'At your age I had girls in and out of my bed all the time.'

Kurt would answer him with a sullen scowl. The boyfriend would shake his head, and Kurt would mentally tell him to fuck off.

Kurt did like girls, though. Underneath his mask of indifference and superiority, he was like any other boy of his age, a ferment of hormones. It was just that he didn't do anything about it. And he certainly wasn't about to do anything to please that jerk who was screwing his mother.

Besides, Kurt was a kind of romantic. Although he had never slept with a girl and was longing to do so, he'd convinced himself that he must fall seriously in love first. But fate behaved toward Kurt as he behaved toward others: it confronted him with something quite different from what he had expected.

Kurt was going through a suicidal phase. It wasn't the first time he'd had such thoughts, but on this particular occasion he made up his mind that if by the end of that month he hadn't succeeded in experiencing what it was like to get laid, he would climb up on the roof and jump off. His chances of meeting this self-imposed condition didn't look good. In fact, he had so few female friends, he had only *one* chance: a girl a couple of years older than him who was somewhat mentally retarded.

One day he stole a bottle of liquor from the super-market and persuaded her to go upstairs with him into his bedroom. After they had drained the whole bottle between the two of them, Kurt put his hand on the girl's breast and fondled it. Without him asking her anything, she started to undress, but the more she undressed the more disgusted he felt – disgusted with himself, with her, and with the whole situation. Especially the situation. He tried to fuck her anyway but couldn't go through with it because the smell of her sex turned his stomach. And as if that wasn't bad enough, his mother came home unexpectedly, having had a quarrel with that same sexist boyfriend, and opened the bedroom door on this terrible scene of her son trying to abuse a mentally disabled girl in her own home. She screamed at him to get out and said she never wanted to see him again.

Kurt fled in despair and kept running all night. The dawn light was like a dagger to his heart. The silence mirrored in the shiny asphalt of the roads was just as painful. His fingers still smelled of the girl. He couldn't shake off his shame at having tried to take advantage of her. It seemed as if that nauseating smell would stay in his nostrils for the rest of his life, that the shame would cling to him forever.

The girl's father came to hear of the way his daughter had been molested. He reported Kurt, who was arrested and questioned, but released because the girl was over eighteen and not mentally retarded according to the legal definition of the term.

But Kurt's exoneration only served to heighten the sense of abandonment and betrayal that had never left him since the day his parents had separated. Now he felt even more guilty and unworthy than he had as a kid. This was the event that led to his roaming the streets of Aberdeen and living under the North Aberdeen Bridge where he and Homer were to meet.

According to Kurt's sister, however, it wasn't true that he slept under that bridge. 'It was all in his imagination,' she said several years later to a biographer in search of unknown details. 'The bridge was just a hangout where he went to smoke pot with his friends. He never slept there.'

'She's right,' confirms Krist, the band's lanky bass player. 'It was all in his imagination. He did hang out there for a while, but that's all. Anyway, you couldn't sleep there on those muddy banks, with the tides coming up and down. That's the way Kurt was. He created himself a past that was worse than it really had been. He was a kind of revisionist. He made up all kinds of things. Once, in the days before we played together, he had this idea of starting a musical fanzine with a guy called Steve. They even produced a kind of pilot issue, but Steve dropped out when he realized Kurt was writing rave reviews of records he'd never listened to. He imagined other things, too. Like when he was still a complete unknown he would write long interviews that he imagined giving to non-existent magazines. He was always saying that he was going to be rich and famous, a rock star, and that at the height of his fame he'd kill himself like Jimi Hendrix. We told him that was stupid talk. But he was very insistent. No, he'd say. I'm going to be a rock star and I'm going to commit suicide by shooting myself in the mouth. When I think about what happened later, I think, fuck! But who'd have imagined he'd really do it? Anyway, Hendrix didn't kill himself. He just died. But we were kids at the time and only knew about him from hearsay.'

So maybe none of it was true. Maybe the story of the retarded girl was only make-believe, Kurt hadn't lived under the North Aberdeen Bridge, and Homer had never met him. Homer himself had his doubts on the matter, if he was really honest. But Kurt was the only person he'd ever trusted. How *could* none of it be true?

Kurt had changed his life. Partly by introducing him to the heroin system, but it wasn't just that. Heroin had changed his life, but the change Homer had in mind affected him as a person. When he was with Kurt, people didn't seem to notice him. For example, he might drop by Kurt's place to collect the usual stuff, and Kurt and Krist would carry on talking about some song that they were going to rehearse or other matters concerning the band. Homer would be there, in front of their eyes, listening intently – even though he wasn't particularly interested in the band's problems – but Krist would take no notice, he would just go on talking, without so much as a glance at Homer. As if he simply wasn't there.

Homer didn't mind too much, since he could never find much to say about subjects like rock or how things were going. Not being involved in the conversation was a blessing to him, in a way. But he couldn't help feeling a little hurt sometimes. For Christ's sake, he'd mutter to himself, I'm not invisible.

Then there was another, even weirder thing. He would be walking along, minding his own business, not going anywhere in particular, and all at once he'd bump into some friend of Kurt's, who would greet him. 'Hi, Kurt,' the friend would say and he'd be startled and flustered and be on the point of telling the friend that he was wrong, that he wasn't Kurt and that he'd mistaken him for Kurt because... But there he would stop, because he didn't have the faintest idea why. So he'd respond to the greeting with a grimace and keep walking, because if he didn't the friend might latch on to him and start asking how he was getting along with his new girlfriend or when he would next be playing with the band around there or other things that Homer wouldn't have been able to answer, since he wasn't Kurt and he'd never met this new girlfriend, though Kurt had talked to him about her for hours on end. Nor would he have been able to say much about the band's plans because, although Kurt always told him every last detail, he just couldn't get his head around their business. So he would just keep walking. Otherwise he would have had to explain why he had responded to the greeting when he wasn't Kurt.

Then there was the fact that Kurt kept calling him Boddah. It's true that that was his middle name, but Homer knew perfectly well that Kurt called him that because of the other Boddah, the childhood friend who had never existed and whom Uncle Clark had wanted to send to Vietnam.

Once Homer put his foot down and demanded that Kurt stop calling him by the name of a person who didn't exist.

'What do you want me to call you, then?' Kurt had asked him.

'Just call me by my own name. Homer.'

'Homer?' Kurt had echoed him, looking dubious.

'Yeah, why? What's wrong with it?'

'It's a hick name.'

'Maybe so, but it's mine.'

'Homer. Never heard of anyone around here with a name like that. This isn't Kentucky,' Kurt had said, as if he was thinking aloud. Homer didn't know what to reply.

'D'you know how far away Kentucky is? Have you ever been there?'

'No.'

'Well, it's a hell of a long way. Besides, it's such a dump, it wouldn't be worth going there even if it was closer than Hoquiam.'

Aberdeen isn't much better, thought Homer. 'Have *you* ever been there?'

'No. In fact I don't see why we're standing here talking about it.'

'I've no idea, Kurt.'

'Neither have I, Boddah,' said Kurt, and burst out laughing. It was one of the few times Homer ever saw Kurt really laugh. Homer started laughing too, but almost at once had a kind of presentiment, a feeling that something was wrong.

Yes, a feeling. Those were the days when he still had feelings. He hadn't yet fallen into his present state of discomfort, then. This sickness so pervasive you couldn't even define it, a sickness that went beyond the pulmonary weakness that had made his life a constant struggle with chronic bronchitis, beyond his intermittent back problems and the assorted side-effects of the medicines he took in a vain attempt to relieve his stomach pain. The terrible, mysterious pain was the worst of his physical ailments, and there was no remedy for it but heroin; only heroin could make him feel better, lull him to sleep, make him forget his stomach and everything else, at least until he woke up and everything started over as if it had never stopped.

Kurt had similar problems. In fact, he had exactly the same problems. Chronic bronchitis, scoliosis, and those stomach pains that the doctors couldn't explain and that made Kurt throw up whatever he ate, even the lightest foods. Like Homer, Kurt seemed to want to do nothing but sleep, because it was only when he slept that he wasn't plagued by his stomach pains and stopped feeling so bad that he wanted to die, though he was still only twenty-four.

They saw less of each other than they used to. Things had started to take off and Kurt was often away on tour with the band. Yet the two of them had never been so alike. Homer found this troubling. He sensed that there was something wrong about it. Yet he avoided discussing it with Kurt, because he was afraid he would think he was crazy. He knew reality wasn't his strong point, he knew how bad he was at assessing situations objectively – he knew all this, because even paranoiacs have their lucid, balanced moments. He tried to reassure himself by supposing that he and Kurt had always been alike, and that the resemblance had escaped him simply because he had never been very observant. He had a hard time recognizing other people's features, even the most noticeable ones, and he wasn't too familiar even with his own appearance. His hair, for example. He wore it long and dirty, as Kurt did, but that didn't mean much, because his state of chronic discomfort certainly didn't leave him any time to think about mundane chores like washing or going to the barber's. The problem was the color. Blond. Since when had his hair been blond like Kurt's? He couldn't remember ever being blond, and yet if he tried to give a color to his hair's past, he couldn't pin-point it; he became like a restless painter dabbling in his palette in search of some impossible hue.

He no longer went to the Laundromat. What was the point, when he never changed his clothes? He always wore the same torn, faded jeans, the same

Converse Chuck Taylors, the same plaid flannel shirt left open over a white T-shirt that sported the slogan HOW ARE YOU?

He had even begun crying. He would cry for no reason, especially if too many hours had passed since his last systemization with heroin. He usually cried when he went walking in the woods, too. It was the sight of the trees. He had a deep affection for those towering, motionless creatures that exuded all the cold and wetness of the earth. Something told him he was about to be separated from them and his heart wept. He was afraid they would all be felled in the end, owls or no owls. He imagined acres of trunks lopped off at the root, amputated stumps shrouded in mist and above them a sky that was grayer than it had ever been before. Tears came to his eyes.

Sometimes he even cried when he opened the fridge. He would open it and just burst into tears. There wasn't much inside it, usually: only a piece of stale cream cheese or a can of flat beer. But that wasn't why he cried. It was just one of those things, there was no reason for it.

All this happened shortly after Kurt told him he thought he might have found love. The girl in question had been showing up at gigs lately and Homer had assumed she was one of the many groupies that followed bands around. Homer only had a vague idea of what these girls were like, because he never went to shows, but he'd heard Krist talk about them once.

'Don't take any notice of what Krist says,' Kurt warned him. 'He doesn't think like us. All he cares about is drinking.' That was nothing unusual in those parts; alcohol was one of the county's main resources and for a certain kind of logger it was even more important than the timber industry. But Krist used to drink himself stupid. 'He gets into a state where he doesn't know what he's doing. Waves his arms about and says things like, You guys know nothing about love,' continued Kurt with that absent expression of his. 'Don't take any notice of him. Anyway, she's not a groupie.' She was the girl they'd seen in *Straight to Hell*, the girl who played in that band from Portland. But for some reason Kurt omitted to mention this detail to Homer.

The girl had sent him a present via Dave, the current drummer. It was a red, love-shaped box. The outside of the box was covered with floral decorations and inside there were pine cones, sea shells, a doll and a miniature tea set. Kurt had been very taken with it and had jotted down on a piece of paper some words that he would later put into one of his songs. I've been locked up for weeks in your love-shaped box, he wrote.

'You know, Homer, it's time you started thinking about love yourself,' said Kurt. Homer didn't reply, but cracked his knuckles pensively. After a while he asked:

'What does a love-shaped box look like?'

220

There were countless things he didn't know about the shape of love, and about women. If ever there was a particle of existence born to live in the dark, that particle was Homer. His interactions with the surrounding world were so weak that he would have walked away with the title of most in-the-dark particle in the universe. The only force to which the particle Homer seemed subject was weak interaction, which would exclude *a priori* any kind of amorous relationship. His interactions with the normal mass of other particles of existence were so weak that they were hardly even aware of his existence. They simply didn't register him, any more than the human ear could distinguish the hum of the accelerated existence of an alien princess from some forbidden planet.

Where was he to begin?

He told himself he would have to find out more about the subject, but he had hardly begun his inquiries when he happened to read that love is by its very nature elusive and becomes downright intractable if you have the impudence to ask it questions like Where do you come from? When are you going to appear?

He read that love was the expression of the emotions, that it was the discovery of bodies and sexual practices. He read the passage in the Bible where it says that love is knowledge, is waking up every morning with a renewed sense of astonishment and wonder. When *he* woke up, the first thing he did was to try to establish whether his stomach pains were still there, and the second was to systemize himself with heroin.

He read about Freud and his theory that everybody's sexuality – and the associated problems – was conditioned by childhood traumas, some imaginary, some real. He read the *Three Essays on the Theory of Sexuality* of 1905 three times, but could find no mention of the problem of body snatchers.

He read about Zelda, a woman who told her husband, a well-known author, that she was intending to write a book about madness. Zelda had been having mental problems lately. Scott – that was the well-known writer's name – flew into a rage because he had already started writing a novel on the same subject. 'You pick up the crumbs from the table where I eat and make books out of them,' Scott said to Zelda. Homer's thoughts wandered to his fridge.

He read that the so-called French kiss, where two partners' mouths open completely to allow their tongues to touch, was already well known in seventeenth-century France, where, however, it was called the Italian kiss. The newspapers confirmed that this kind of kiss was still prevalent in Italy even today, so much so in fact that the Italian highway code included a clause specifically forbidding drivers to execute it at the wheel. There were some people, however, who wanted to ban the disgusting habit of people touching each other with their lips in all circumstances, on the grounds that a kiss attracts more germs than a fly-strip attracts flies. Homer's thoughts wandered to the fly-strips that hung from the ceiling of Kurt's apartment in Olympia.

He read the last sentence of a book called *Gone With the Wind*. The sentence ran, 'Tomorrow is another day.' Homer's thoughts this time remained completely blank.

He read about a gynecologist and a psychologist, William Masters and Virginia Johnson, who, after observing more than ten thousand sex acts in their laboratory in St Louis, Missouri, came to the conclusion that American citizens quite simply did not know how to make love. Homer frowned inwardly.

One day when he was in the store he happened to glance at a shelf where there were a couple of those magazines that specialize in photographs of female bodies. He took one and opened it. He saw a girl looking out at him from a photograph that occupied a whole page. She was naked and was leaning against the trunk of a palm tree. Behind her was the blue backdrop of the sea. There was also a caption. 'Spring,' ran the caption. 'At this joyous time of year when everything comes back to life and the cold, rainy days are behind us, all of us feel the urge to head for a nice sunny beach.' Homer looked out of the store window, saw that it had not in fact stopped raining at all, looked thoughtful without thinking about anything in particular, and read on. 'But is that really what makes us want to go there? Or is it the hope, the desire, to see – after ten long months – a lot of beautiful bodies basking in the sun?' Homer asked himself the same question and read on. 'Look at the photograph of this gorgeous girl, for example.' Homer had already looked, but now did so again, more attentively. 'Look how she flaunts her youthfulness, her beautiful body, without the least inhibition.' Homer put the magazine back on the shelf because the store proprietor was eying him, and went out.

The next day he went back to the store and bought a book. The title was *A Manual of Man-to-Woman Conversation.* He bought it because he had seen a book of this kind at Kurt's house: *All You Need To Know About the Music Business.* Admittedly, it was on a different subject. But where was the harm in trying?

The book fell into three sections: the basic grammar, the sure-fire phrases, the danger words. Homer thought it might provide him with some useful hints. When he got home he slumped on the couch, took some heroin and started leafing through his new acquisition. The television was on and was showing footage of an African-American citizen being beaten up by six police officers in California. He opened a page at random. 'Sex is a tricky game,' said the random page. 'For example, if you tell a woman you want to make love to her she might think you don't care what *she* wants to do. What you must do is get her interested by other means, show her you haven't forgotten it takes two to make love.' The random page did not, however, specify what these other means were. Nor did the next page. Homer chucked the book aside and watched the police officers laying into the African-American citizen.

On April 6th 1991, Kurt called Homer and told him he and his band were on the point of signing a contract with a major label to record a new album. He said they were going to Los Angeles next month for the recording sessions. Homer's comment on the news was the one he frequently made on such matters: 'Huh?'

Kurt explained to him how important the whole venture was and that it could be the chance of a lifetime. He sounded happy. Happy in that way of his that always made it seem as if he didn't give a shit about anything, because nothing could change things or make him feel better. Kurt also told him he was going to be away for quite a while, so Homer had better get himself organized, a clear hint that, as far as the system was concerned, he was going to have to provide for himself. Homer replied that he wouldn't be needing anything for a while.

The truth was that Kurt had been away often recently. Since things had begun to happen, the band had been traveling a lot; they had even done a tour of

Europe. Something was changing: the band was leaving the underground world of indie rock to enter a new one. Homer sensed that there was a certain conflict between Kurt's concept of music and the contract he had just signed with the major label; he was afraid Kurt might vanish, as he had done once before in the early days. He had been worrying about this for some time, and had begun to take precautions. Every time

he went to see Kurt to buy some powdered system, he made sure the quantity was greater than he needed, sometimes even twice as much. In practice, it was the same technique as he'd used with his space toys when he was a kid. When he got home, he would wrap the excess baggies in tin foil and then further protect them with duct tape. Then he'd pack them into a base-ball, in which he had cut a special access hole. Homer was no baseball fan, but he'd had this idea while watching some film in which a batter hammered the ball over the grandstand and hit the electronic score-board, which showered the spectators with a sputter-ing cascade of sparks, like fireworks on the Fourth of July. When he saw those pictures Homer realized that his name wasn't just a hick name, as Kurt had said. It also meant a home run. And he thought of buying a baseball to hide his store of system in.

The solution was practical, because a baseball could be put almost anywhere and even carried around, if need be. Moreover, as an object it had a peculiar beauty of its own and was a pleasure to hold in the hand. Sometimes he would pick up his bulging baseball, thinking of the time when he would inhale all the heroin that was inside it. He would hold it to his nose and sniff the smell of the leather. At other times he would turn it over in his hands, running his thumbs along the seams. He spent so long caressing it that before the week was out it had lost its shine. Even an expert player would scarcely have believed that it had never seen a baseball field in its life. It even seemed to bear the marks of repeated hits, because Homer often took it with him on his walks through the woods and hurled it against the tree trunks.

'I'll be okay for a while,' repeated Homer. Kurt said he was glad and suggested Homer take a trip to California to visit him during the recordings. 'Fuck it, Boddah, you've seen nothing but trees and loggers all your life. Maybe you ought to start seeing something of the world apart from Aberdeen and Olympia.'

Homer's only reply was a sort of grunt. But the idea appealed to him, because the question of love had given him a yearning to visit the places he had seen on TV, an itch to leave home, even though the years had strangely tied him to the place where he'd grown up. Often he felt tired of all that rain, often he would have given anything just to see two consecutive sunny days, often the uncouthness of the people was more than he could stand, often he wished he lived in a town where people had higher ambitions, where kids dreamed of something better than a job in a service station or a lumberyard. He wished he could live in another town, because in the one where he was born the people gathered on Sundays in parking lots to turn them into swap meets, where women tried to raise a few bucks by selling the overcooked food they'd prepared at home before daybreak; miserable gatherings where people brought junk they had fished out of their cellars in the hope that some gullible fool might buy it; trading posts where some relic of a comfortable life of dirt and poverty would pass to another comfortable life of dirt and poverty; markets where the only wares on sale were the disappointments people kept close to their hearts, like cigarette packets tucked in their shirt pockets.

But somewhere, perhaps not too far from Grays Harbor County, there must be an America that was truly different, more like the America Homer had glimpsed in his favorite pieces of film, an America where you could sleep without having to integrate yourself into the system. Another world.

5.

Independent Days

The stains of a red Californian sunset had just faded from the sky, and huge trucks charged along the roads, trumpeting like some new species of pachyderm asserting their territorial claims over the night.

The Sound City studios, where Kurt and the band were recording their album, were at Van Nuys, in the San Fernando Valley. In 1991 everything was going digital and the Los Angeles bands wanted studios that could offer state-of-the-art equipment, not an antiquated Seventies recording console with an imitation wood panel. Sound City was a relic of a different age. It had the smell of decay about it, a smell very similar to that of nostalgia. It wouldn't be long, that smell seemed to say, before the studios closed.

Homer arrived there by taxi from the bus station. He didn't notice the sign restricting entry to clients and personnel only, and entered without ringing the bell, because the door was open. He walked down a corridor and came to a little lounge with a couple of dingy brown sofas and a soda machine that was probably out of order. There was no sign of life. Only silence, which did not tally with Homer's idea of a recording studio.

He walked some way without meeting anyone, until he reached the control booth of the main studio, Studio A, where he found a guy gazing pensively through the large horizontal glass that gave onto the recording room. Homer approached the mixing board and looked out too. He saw a large room whose walls were decorated with a brightly colored mural of the Los Angeles skyline. The ceiling was covered with white sound baffles, and the dingy brown color of the old carpet recalled the two shabby sofas in the lounge. A bewildering tangle of cords connected mikes, amps, instruments and effects pedals. The floor was covered with a forest of metal rods among which the cords snaked; music stands and stools were scattered all around and candles – Kurt was very fond of candles – were everywhere. Dave the new drummer's kit was there, and a black piano stood in a corner, near the glass of the control room. The piano had been brought in just in case, but during those six weeks of recording it languished in its corner, gathering dust.

On the wall behind the drums was a clock. Homer wondered if the noise of the hands disturbed the recordings. He was about to drift off into a reverie on time, on the years that had passed since he had met Kurt under the bridge in Aberdeen, and on all the miles he had traveled by bus to get there, when his eye fell on a smashed guitar lying on the floor. It was part of the arsenal of guitars that Kurt had brought with him, a real collector's item, a left-handed Mosrite. Kurt was a lefty; Homer couldn't tell one hand from the other.

'We're through for today,' said the man. 'That was the only left-handed guitar available.' The rest of Kurt's arsenal, a Sixties Mustang, a Jaguar with DiMarzio pickups, an old Stella acoustic and some new Stratocasters, had been left in the apartment complex where the band were staying.

Kurt wasn't new to such exploits. Sometimes while he was playing he would suddenly fly into a rage and smash his guitar. He was getting a reputation for it. He had started years ago, when he used to get furious at the band's first drummer, who was fond of alcohol. The guy would begin drinking as soon as he arrived at rehearsals, and after half an hour would be so wasted he couldn't go on. Kurt would start slamming his guitar on the ground in frustration, hammer away till he broke it, then hurl it at the drums. Or even at the drummer, if things had gone particularly badly.

On that day, May 2nd 1991, the band's first day of recording at Sound City, they had been planning to record a song they thought would be the album's first hit. At first the mood had been relaxed, and it had looked like things were going to go well, but then the tension rose. After a third unsuccessful try at the song, they'd started jamming freely, as they usually did in such circumstances. Kurt had loosened the strings of his guitar and flailed away, while Krist and Dave tried to keep up with him. But still the sound hadn't improved, so Kurt had started smashing his guitar and screaming incoherently into the mike.

Homer was listening to all that noise now, because the guy at the mixing desk had started playing back the tape. You could hear the dying moans of the shattered guitar. 'What are we going to do with this stuff?' the man said.

'You could use it,' suggested Homer.

The man turned to look at him. They had never met before, but Homer knew he was a calm, laidback guy called Butch, the producer of the album. Kurt had mentioned him once or twice, because he'd worked with him the previous year on some sessions for the band's old indie label. Butch had a reputation as an independent producer who only worked with bands he liked. He knew how to turn the raucous ferocity of punk musicians into a clean, honest sound.

'You think so?'

'You could put it at the end of the album.'

'Make it the last song?'

'In a way, but that wasn't exactly what I meant.'

'No?' said Butch, eying Homer, and showing no sign of surprise at the appearance of this intruder in the studios.

'I was thinking of something more invisible. A ghost track.' He remembered a trick that Kurt had been fond of playing when he was younger. You take a blank ninety-minute cassette and wind it through nearly to the end, and there you record yourself saying some menacing phrases in a scary voice. Then some time afterward, when you're spending the night with a girl, you secretly start the cassette, so that an hour and a half later this voice suddenly whispers, 'I'm coming to get you.' The girl jumps and says, 'Hey, did you hear that?' Whereupon the prankster chuckles to himself and says: 'Hear *what*?' It can be a lot of fun, if you have a suitable girl on hand.

'A ghost track, you say.'

'Yeah,' said Homer, as if Butch, too, knew all about Kurt's prank.

Later Butch discussed it with the band and they all thought it was a great idea. They decided to put the song at the end of the album, a sudden explosion of noise ten minutes after the last song had faded out. It would be very effective with the new CD format. But owing to a technical error it wasn't included on the first pressing of the album.

'Where is everyone?' asked Homer.

Butch, who was still mulling over the idea of the ghost track, jerked his head toward the smashed guitar on the other side of the window, to remind him of the problem.

'Is there a Motel 6 around here?'

'Why?'

'I need a room,' explained Homer.

'What for?'

'I need to relax for a while.'

Butch stared at him.

'Everybody knows what it feels like after days of vibration on wheels to suddenly lie in still beds on still ground and sleep,' said Homer. Butch didn't reply.

'Kerouac wrote that. Jack Kerouac. He was a writer of

handbooks on road travel. I borrowed some of them from the library in Aberdeen. That's where I come from.'

'Yeah, I know,' said Butch. Then he remembered the question Homer had asked him. 'There's a Holiday Inn right behind here. The truckers use it.' He looked puzzled, as if he found it strange that Homer should need a room.

'No Motel 6?'

'Not around here, as far as I know.'

'Well, it'll do for one night. I'll look for one tomorrow,' Homer mused, almost to himself.

'Why a Motel 6?' asked Butch, after a few moments' hesitation.

'They leave the light on for you,' explained Homer in the tone of someone answering a particularly stupid question. And so saying, he went out, swinging his duffel bag over his shoulder.

'Everything okay, Kurt?' asked Butch when Homer had already gone. 'Hey, get a grip on yourself, man,' Butch said to himself. He glanced once more at the wrecked guitar. Then he switched off the equipment and left.

Although he'd only been on the road for two weeks, he'd already formed some regular habits. In the evening he'd get off at the bus station in some town or other, take a room in a nearby motel, preferably a Motel 6, and once he was safely hidden from prying eyes, take the sacred baseball out of his bag, remove the dowel that he used as a stopper, extract one of the bags, systemize himself with heroin, switch on the television and lie down on the bed fully clothed to stare at the ceiling for half an hour or so, thinking about the things he'd seen from the bus window, or some girl who'd got on during the journey. Then he'd go out to buy some fried chicken, return to the motel, eat the fried chicken, systemize himself with heroin again and go out a second time, smelling of fried fat, to have a drink in some bar, where he'd stare at the counter thinking about the same things he'd thought about two hours earlier, staring at the ceiling of his room.

In the morning he'd have breakfast, pay the bill for his room, deposit his duffel bag – with the baseball inside it – in a coin-operated locker at the bus station, check the timetable and stroll around town till it was time to get on the bus and set off on his journey again. Miles of being gently rocked to and fro on a seat, preferably at the back of the bus. Miles of signs showing names that had been given to places and numbers indicating the distances between them, of skies that changed color, of electricity pylons, of black cables along which electricity raced at the speed of light, of billboards, of oncoming trucks trumpeting their horns as they flashed by, of roadside scrub, of squeaky seats, of sighs and groans of people getting off and on en route to their mysterious destinations, of desolate bus stations in the midst of the void of an endless America.

He avoided traveling at night. When the sun was about to set, he'd get off at the first stop, no matter where it was, no matter how dismal the surroundings. The important thing was that there be a motel nearby – and there always was one near the bus station. The important thing was not to travel at night. He was afraid the rocking of the bus might lull him to sleep and that he would lose control of the situation. He needed the warmth of a safe place where he could open his bag and take out his baseball, and he had found that warmth in the Motel 6 motels. Clean comfortable rooms, a bed with a firm mattress, a bathroom with two bars of soap, two towels, two plastic cups and a roll of toilet paper. Local phonecalls free; no additional charges for long distance and international calls; fax and free coffee machine in the lobby.

The bare necessities at an affordable price – and price was a crucial consideration for the guests of Motel 6; for they were the kind of travelers who calculated their bills down to the last cent, who couldn't claim traveling expenses or deduct them from tax. Travelers like Homer, who, when he saw that red six against the blue background, felt almost at home, because he remembered what Tom Bodett always said on the radio, that that sign in the colors of the national flag had been left on for you.

In some ways it was almost better than being at home, for in their very indistinguishability from one another, in their way of being so inconceivably identical over miles of distance, the rooms of Motel 6 provided a refuge, a momentary respite, but also a continuation of that constant sense of being on the run that was shared by all travelers of the American roads. In those identical rooms, Homer, and others like him, could momentarily escape the boundaries imposed by the world, boundaries dictated by things that were only apparently obvious, such as the fact of being men rather than women, boundaries that marked off accessible spaces and uncrossable thresholds such as the men's and women's restrooms, boundaries that fixed the way you furnished your house, the style of clothes you wore, the shape of the objects you bought, the words you used in particular circumstances, the food you ordered in restaurants. Boundaries that seemed to disappear in the rooms of Motel 6, where the smell and shape of the soap bar on the basin were always the same, with no distinction between man and woman; rooms that represented a night of suspended immobility beside the roads, where the cars continued to rush past, shining their headlamps into the darkness; democratic islands of anonymity where there was no place for differents.

Then there was the fascination of that number. It seemed to encapsulate the spirit of an entire people, of citizens who found in the minimal geography of motel rooms the best they could possibly ask of the great consumer society in which they had the good fortune to live. Motel 6 – behind that simple name lay the mystery, the nostalgic appeal of an age that was not too distant but of which all knowledge had been lost, the Sixties, when the Motel Sixes had been given their name because the average price of a room was only six dollars sixty. Now that the cost of living had multiplied threefold, and in some cases even four- and fivefold, that red six against a blue background had become an abstract number which no longer corresponded to any reality and so had taken on a new meaning, as a symbol for initiates, a coded signal that stayed on all night for those travelers of the road who were able to grasp its essence, its being part of a world that, in the small ghost towns of the American provinces, was not yet dead.

He had been on the road for just over two weeks. After Kurt's phonecall suggesting he join him in California during the recording sessions for the new album, it had taken him about ten days to bring himself to leave the no-hope town where he'd always lived. He'd been deterred by his state of chronic discomfort; he'd feared he wouldn't have the strength to leave his home and his trees, to live a life where he would always have to be self-possessed, always ready to deal with situations. But a sudden awareness of all the time that had passed, that he didn't have much time left and that soon he would be in a state where all he could do was wait for the end, the idea that he ought to gamble the little strength he still had, and the mirages of glamorous girls who looked out at him from the covers of the magazines in the store – all these considerations had eventually prevailed.

He'd called a couple of his best customers to

explain that he intended to clear his whole stock of space toys, and before the week was out his mailbox had been overflowing with checks. In a few days he sold off to the nostalgia geeks all the treasures he'd sealed up and stored away in his unhappy childhood years. He had nothing left now, except a tidy sum of money and his priceless baseball, which he put into an old duffel bag along with some other things that he picked up more or less at random around the house, without stopping to think seriously about what he would need when he was traveling.

He had turned out the lights, taken the phone off the hook and laid it on the floor. He had gone toward the front door with his bag slung over his shoulder, turning in the doorway for one final look at the past. He had glanced at the couch and the coffee table and the TV with the dusty pile of videos on top of it. He had felt a pang of heartache. Then he had shut the door behind him, and set off for the bus station, almost sure he would never return, almost sure he would find something along the way; almost happy. An almost-happiness made up of suffused anguish and the conviction that he could face the unknown; the feeling that he was almost alive, that he really existed.

* * *

The original plan was for three weeks' recording. More than a month passed: the band and the others were still in Van Nuys, struggling with Kurt's songs.

The sessions were pretty relaxed, but although Butch tried to avoid putting pressure on the band and on Kurt in particular – having noticed how moody and depressive he was – there were still some minor problems to solve. One was that Kurt had started recording the album before he'd finished the lyrics.

Some days they would all meet in the studios and just stand around watching Kurt scribbling in his notebook, its crumpled pages covered with crossings-out, with precarious words written in a tentative, shaky hand, doomed to eventual deletion. It was a surreal situation: an entire recording studio in total silence, except for Krist, who would be tapping his foot and sighing loudly so that Kurt would hear him.

Now and again Kurt would raise his head and look around. He would meet someone's staring eyes, return to his lyrics, write a few words – a line at most – stop and look around again. He was constantly sweating, but not because of the tension. They were in Los Angeles, after all, and the band was used to a very different climate. Besides, Kurt didn't know any dealers there, and as everyone knows, withdrawal is in itself a form of tension severe enough to make you sweat. It's true that he could have asked Homer for some of the heroin stored in his baseball, but for some reason he didn't, trying instead to get by on codeine-based cough syrup. This had the incidental advantage of preserving his voice, which was always giving out, usually just when the time came to record the vocal tracks.

As soon as he had decided on the finished lyrics, Kurt would start singing at such a raucous pitch that his throat got sore and he had to stop after a couple of verses. Butch contrived to use any sound he could get out of him, because he knew how hard it was to convince him to do a second take. This wasn't just because Kurt was afraid of losing his voice; in his punk view of the world, you had to do things right away, and once you'd done them you had to move on to something else.

Butch, too, had a punk idea of the album: he wanted a loud, intense sound, like that which the band generated in live performance. This required some intricate production work, like doubletracking the guitars, using multiple mikes and finding ways of expanding the sound mass, until it seemed like a pulsing body in search of an outlet, filling every cubic inch of available space. The use of such technical devices went against the grain with Kurt, but Butch was careful not to push him too far. Kurt was suspicious by nature – not quite as bad as Homer, but still very suspicious. The more you tried to convince him of something, the more skeptical and irritable he became, until eventually he'd just say no. 'I don't want to do it anymore,' he would say, shaking his head, and Butch would know it was no use arguing because the kid had retreated into his shell and he wasn't going to get anything else out of him.

Unlike Krist, who was outgoing and joked with everybody, Kurt kept aloof from all the discussions about what to do and how to do it. The abiding image of those weeks in Van Nuys was of Kurt hunched up on one of the shabby brown sofas, brooding on thoughts that he confided to no one.

On the first day, when the band arrived at the studios, Krist had been impressed by the numerous gold and platinum record awards hanging on the walls, and by the names of the great musicians who had recorded at Sound City in the Seventies, dinosaurs of rock history. Kurt, however, had merely remarked that the mixing board smelled old, like everything else in the place, from the carpet upward. That was where Kurt differed from Krist and from the rest of humanity: where they saw the beginning of something, he only saw its end. This was not insensitivity or cynicism on his part, it was just that he was physically affected by certain smells, such as that of the dust that could swamp a brown carpet and turn it an indiscriminate gray.

He saw neglect – not the mere carelessness of lazy, slipshod, selfish people, but universal neglect. This, to him, was the supreme force that was going to take over, sooner or later. The world was heading down a path from a point where there was something to a point where there would be nothing. Dust would prevail in the end, whatever happened.

This notion of life crumbling from neglect explained why Kurt's lyrics were full of violent juxtapositions and dyslexic plans, such as planting houses or building trees; it explained why his songs were always full of pain and why they sounded screamed even when he sang them quietly; perhaps it also explained the hoarseness of his voice: because the words, *those* words, rasped his throat like sandpaper.

One day one of the sound technicians asked Kurt what his songs were about. 'I don't understand them,' said the technician. 'That teenage deodorant song, for example. Man, it's strong stuff. I *feel* that it means something, but I don't know what.' In truth, Kurt's lyrics never had a precise meaning. Sometimes they had no meaning at all, or if they did have one it was unintentional. They were just lyrics. They were written that way because they sounded good, because they were cool to sing.

Kurt watched Homer checking the candles scattered over the studio floor. This was the job Homer had taken upon himself – relighting the candles that went out, and replacing those that were burning low. Apart from this he kept in the background, never saying a word. The smell of wax was so strong it was soporific.

'It's about alienation, I guess,' replied Kurt.

The technician would have liked to know more, to understand more clearly, but was afraid of being thought stupid if he persisted. It wasn't done to ask about the precise meaning of things.

'I don't know. There's never any real theme. Usually I pick the words up here and there, stealing them from things I've already written.' He paused. 'I'm imperfect. You know what I mean?'

The sound technician bit his lower lip, his face a picture of blank intensity. They were sitting on one of the brown sofas in the lounge.

'It's about friends,' explained Kurt, meaning the deodorant song. 'About the friends I have now, who are the same kind of friends we have when we're teenagers. And about wanting to break things, write on walls and overturn beds, to change things by just saying no. It's the way I feel.'

'Like a teenager, you mean?'

He tried to say yes, but his stomach was hurting and he could hardly breathe for the burning in his throat. A teenager doesn't feel this bad, he thought. He wants to smash things, and he feels bad, but he never has stomach pains.

'Growing up without becoming an adult, that's what I meant,' he said at length, taking a shot from the bottle of Jack Daniel's that he gripped between his legs. His face contracted in a grimace of pain and the sound technician was tempted to ask why he drank all that whiskey in his condition. But he didn't, because that, too, was a forbidden subject. Kurt gasped for breath and stared fixedly in front of him, his eyes veiled by a gelatinous patina, as if they were full of tears.

The technician smoothed down the thighs of his jeans and stood up. 'I've got to get back to Butch.'

Kurt sat quite still, his expression vacant, as if he hadn't heard. 'Sure,' he said after a few seconds, when the technician had already left. Then he fell asleep on the sofa. His head lolled forward, but the bottle of Jack Daniel's remained miraculously upright.

*   *   *

Memorial Day 1991 finally came around. They decided to celebrate with an old-fashioned barbecue in the parking lot outside Studio A.

It was one of those late spring days when the sky is paled by carbon monoxide, and the calm of the secluded neighborhood around Sound City was deepened by a holiday stupor. Even the chicken roasting on the grill smelled of drowsiness.

As they waited to get their hands on the greasy meat, the sleepy participants in the feast wandered around the parking lot with a strange anguish in their hearts and a can of beer in their hands. Now and then their thoughts would turn to the headquarters of some of the larger porno film companies, near the studios. Kurt remembered the Community World Theater in Tacoma, where the band had done their first big show. Poorly heated and reeking of urine, it was a converted porno house.

Perhaps he also thought back to their very first gig, in Raymond, a logging town half an hour's drive from Aberdeen.

'Shit,' Kurt had exclaimed that day. 'Those guys probably don't even know what radio is yet. It'll be a flop, I just know it will. They're going to hate us.' Although it was an eventful evening, it actually went better than expected. Some people almost congratulated them. 'You guys aren't half bad, after all,' one person said.

A pretty young woman had gone up to Kurt to ask him the lyrics of a song they'd played. She'd gotten the idea that Kurt had made up the words on the spot, inspired by her shining blonde hair. He hadn't; the song was about how much he loathed heavy metal. And if there was another thing he loathed it was people misinterpreting his lyrics.

'You really want to know?' Kurt asked her, with a scowl.

She smiled at him pleadingly, and he said: 'It goes something like this: fuck, cunt, cocksucker, shit-eater, bitch, son of a bitch, anal prober.'

Those were the early days, when Kurt used to send dozens of tapes of the band to the record labels, accompanied by inflated CVs and letters that always ended more or less like this: 'Listen, guys. We are willing to pay for the pressing of the first 1,000 copies of our LP, and all the recording costs. We basically just want to be on your label. We want it that fucking bad. But if you really think we suck, could you PLEASE send us a reply of NOT INTERESTED, or whatever other formula you use in such cases? You can even be more explicit if you want. Like, TAKE YOUR CRAPPY MUSIC AND FUCK OFF. Feel free to express yourselves. That way we won't send you any more tapes. You'll have a quieter life and we won't waste our money.'

It was sad to remember these things, now that they were finally recording for a major, now that they were standing there discussing the album and speculating about its prospects.

They all agreed that it was powerful stuff, that it might do well.

The band were due to leave Van Nuys two weeks later for an eight-gig tour of the West Coast, and the owners of the apartment complex where they were staying would probably be glad to see the back of them. They would come home at six o'clock in the morning every day, turn all the couches upside down and spray-paint the walls with graffiti until they looked like the inside of a subway car.

This wasn't just a national holiday, it was a farewell party for two friends who were about to go their separate ways.

'Things are going to change, Boddah,' said Kurt to Homer.

'I know,' said Homer.

'Nothing will be the same anymore.'

Homer didn't reply.

'You know what the best time for a band is?'

Homer shook his head.

'Right before they become famous.' There was a tinge of sadness in his words.

'Are *you* going to be famous?'

'Once that happens, whatever you play they turn it into pretty girls in skimpy clothes surrounded by dry ice. You know what I mean?'

Homer thought he might be talking about rock videos, but wasn't sure.

'I'm afraid this is one of the few good times of my life and that it's not going to last long.' Kurt paused. 'They'll add a couple of guys in flannel shirts, a few tattoos, and some anarchy symbols.'

'To the girls and the dry ice, you mean?'

'That's all that'll be left of what we're doing now. Flannel shirts and anarchy symbols. Zilch.' He put his arms across his abdomen and bent forward, uttering a noise that reminded Homer of the way aliens talk. One of his attacks of stomach cramp. His eyes watered from the pain. 'D'you think it's possible to die of stomach ache?' said Kurt, trying to get his breath back.

Homer thought about it. 'I guess so.'

'Shit,' said Kurt, gazing vaguely in the direction of

Krist, Dave and all the others. They were standing around the barbecue, slapping each other on the back and laughing raucously. 'One evening, before a show, I felt ill. There was this burning in my stomach and I was suffering from flu. It was like I'd felt that way forever. It was so bad I couldn't even cough – as soon as I started coughing I felt like throwing up. In the end I *did* throw up into a garbage can, and one of the staff called a doctor.'

Homer nodded to indicate that he was following.

'I was still throwing up into the garbage can when the doctor arrived. He looked at me, but kept well back. Someone told him about my stomach pains, and he put on a there's-no-need-to-explain-anything-to-me-I'm-a-doctor kind of air. He just stood there watching me spew, and didn't do a fucking thing.'

Homer waited for him to go on.

'That's all there is to tell. He went away, and that was that. He stood around for a while, did fuck all, and left.'

'I get those stomach pains too, and all those other things,' said Homer.

'I know, Boddah. I know.' He looked around, like he was searching for something that wasn't there.

For a few moments all sound vanished from the

parking lot. It was as if the barbecue were taking place behind the glass of a fishbowl. With an effort Homer broke the silence. 'I'm leaving, Kurt.'

'Are you going home?'

'No.'

'Where are you going, then?'

'Further south. Then on to Nevada.'

'Doing a little tour of your own, huh?' said Kurt. He giggled nervously at his joke and huddled his shoulders as if he were cold. But it was late May and the California sun was warm. 'It's because of that love thing, isn't it?'

'Yeah.'

'Sure. You're doing the right thing, you know?'

'There's a place in Nevada called Rachel. That's where I'm going.'

'You're going to look for love in Rachel, Nevada?'

'Well, in actual fact, it's a place that doesn't exist. Flying saucers land nearby and there's a reception area for aliens. I don't know whether they're like us or different, but it's the only place I can think of to go and look.'

'The body snatchers might catch up with you.'

'I know,' said Homer solemnly. 'But I'll be ready for them.' He showed Kurt his baseball.

Neither of them said so, but they both thought back to the night they'd met. One of the songs on the album was about the time Kurt had spent under the bridge in Aberdeen. It had only been a brief experience, but while it was happening Kurt had imagined he was really homeless and so ill he couldn't move. He had even imagined he had the new immune-deficiency virus. When he thought back to that period, it seemed like pure fantasy, but if he compared it to what he had become now and to the way he felt, the nights spent under that wood-and-concrete structure that spanned the river Wishkah seemed to sum up his inability to cope with life. People were always asking him, 'Why the hell are you depressed?' He almost always gave the same reply – except when he just stared back, with a fuck-you expression on his face. His reply was: 'Because I'm *awake*. Why else?' He had become a narcoleptic. He liked sleeping. He adored sleeping. He'd fall asleep when he was bored, on the van, when he was traveling with the band. In front of the TV, of course, and sometimes even in the middle of a meal. Whenever he encountered something or someone he couldn't face up to, he'd sleep all day. His ideal life was a comatose state that you only awoke from to go and play rock music. He preferred to stay shut up in his own little world rather than venture out into the big world of others. Sleep was also a way of dealing with his stomach pain. When he was asleep he forgot he had a stomach; when he awoke he cursed the fact that he was still alive, so acute was the pain.

Five and a half years had passed since his time as an immune-deficient bum. A short time, really, but his total loss of hope, his lack of anything to say anymore, made it seem like an arc that spanned a whole life. He felt guilty for feeling the way he did, for his indifference to the little pleasures people settled for, like spending an hour just chatting with friends.

'Rachel. Wasn't that the name of the replicant in *Blade Runner*?' Kurt asked.

'Yeah.'

They both fell silent, pondering that meaningless coincidence. Recently Kurt had taken to wearing pajamas in the daytime. The ones he had on now were made of blue plaid, like those he would wear at his wedding in Hawaii the following year. He was also wearing a beret, sandals and a Guatamalan purse. Homer's clothing was the same as ever.

'Well, I hope things work out for you down there,' said Kurt.

Homer grimaced wryly.

'So you finally left home to see this great country of ours,' said Kurt, lighting one of his self-rolled cigarettes. 'You know, when I was a kid the United States seemed so big to me, I thought I'd never leave the county.' He paused to take a first drag. 'I dreamed of being president – without ever leaving a godforsaken little town in the Northwest.' He coughed. 'Things can be much simpler when you're small,' he said with a sigh.

'Yeah.'

'And very complicated.'

'Yeah.'

'When I was nine I thought I'd never reach age twenty-one. I've made it to twenty-four.' He chuckled. 'Sometimes I just can't get over it. I can't believe it, you know? My life's always been like that: when I was small I thought I was just an ordinary kid, then my parents split up and I found myself living with my father in a fucking trailer. I liked the Beatles, not knowing they'd broken up years before. I was all keyed up to go and see them live, but they hadn't played together for ages. Same thing with Led Zeppelin. They'd broken up long before I started listening to them too. We're a bunch of punk rockers who missed out on the punk era, because by the time we started it was over. And all because we had parents who drank and fucked around. And got divorced.'

Homer listened, thinking of the past, of the moment

when he'd realized that his mother had changed, that she was different. Life had been hard. For both of them – him and Kurt.

'It would take a really terrible experience to give me back the enthusiasm I had when I was a kid. Like cutting myself on a piece of rusty old iron and getting tetanus,' Kurt went on.

'I've got to go.'

'Sure,' said Kurt, clapping his hands. 'Maybe I'm just a little wuss, whining because he doesn't want to grow up. What do you think?'

'I don't know, Kurt.' And he really didn't.

Kurt took off his beret and fit it on Homer's head. Then he clasped Homer's shoulders and said: 'Well, looks like we won't be seeing each other for a while.'

Homer lowered his gaze. He couldn't bear to mirror himself in the sadness of Kurt's steel-colored eyes.

'Be careful with that ball you carry around with you.' Kurt released his friend's shoulders and took a couple of steps back. Homer turned and set off, head hung low, toward Cabrito Road and the other roads he would have to travel before he reached Nevada. He had almost reached the end of the parking lot when from a distance Kurt said to him: 'I'll write to you some day, when it's all over.' But he said it in a voice too broken

for Homer to hear him. Finally, when Homer had disappeared from sight and he was still standing there in
his blue plaid pajamas, he said, in a whisper that
wasn't even a breath: 'Boddah.'

The air smelled of grilled chicken that day.

6.

Smalltown Ghost

There is another possibility.

Perhaps the question of love wasn't a question at all. Nor a firefly, one of those spectral clouds that had materialized in the icy skies of the North at the close of the second millennium.

Perhaps the need for love appeared to Homer in the form of light. Not just an ordinary light, that is. But an unexpected gleam that appears where there should have been the thickest fog or the deepest gloom or the blackest despair. The kind of light you think you see on the horizon, bright against the backcloth of the night, ready to perform unusual optical pirouettes, and you cry out: 'Hey, did you see that?'

'See what?'

'That stuff over there.'

'Over where?'

'Against the backcloth of the night.'

'That light, you mean?'

'Yeah, that's it. But I don't think it's just a light.'

'You don't?'

'Look how it moves. A normal light can't do that kind of thing.'

'No.'

'I've never seen such unusual optical pirouettes.'

'Neither have I.'

'Wow, what a sight.'

'Yeah.'

'What do you think it is?'

'What do *you* think?'

'I've no idea.'

'Looks like a light to me.'

'Oh, come on.'

'I don't see what else it could be.'

'I guess you're right.'

'Sure I'm right. Look.'

'I am looking.'

'Well?'

'A light. I think it's a light.'

'No shit.'

'It's definitely a light.'

'Although. . .'

'Although what?'

'Doesn't it look a bit strange to you, for a light?'

'Yeah.'

'Suppose it's not a light.'

'Suppose.'

'It could be anything.'

'It could.'

'Like what?'

'I can't think of anything.'

'Neither can I.'

'You know what?'

'What?'

'I say it's a light and to hell with it.'

'Me too.'

'What do you say we quit asking each other questions and go to bed?'

'All right. But we go to bed, period.'

'What do you mean, period?'

'I mean we just sleep.'

'What about love?'

'Hey! What have you got in mind?'

'Nothing. It's just that I thought. . .'

'Fuck what you thought. You weren't thinking you could use this light thing. . .'

'Oh well, I tried.'

'And you failed. I don't give a shit about lights.'

'But I love you.'

'Go tell that to some other girl.'

'I really do.'

'Well, I don't love you.'

'Not even a little?'

'Listen, just stop bugging me and turn out the light.'

WELCOME TO RACHEL

Population

Humans 98   Aliens ?

Many years ago a hunter of white whales said that real places were never marked on maps. He was right, for many maps of Nevada didn't show Rachel. They did show Tempiute, but not Rachel. Tempiute was a mountain five miles east of Rachel. Once there had been a tungsten mine there, but now it was abandoned. The people of Rachel hoped Union Carbide would come and reopen the mine some day, but it was a pretty forlorn hope.

After the closure of the mine, around 1988, half the population of Rachel reluctantly decided to leave the town and the arid, sandy area where it was situated, the Sand Springs Valley. Fewer than a hundred people stayed: a few hardy pioneers who loved the heroic, empty freedom of the frontier towns, lucky folk who didn't need to work for a living, had some savings in the bank and thought buying five acres of desert for the moderate sum of six thousand five hundred dollars was a bargain. And it did make a nice little property. You put in a mobile home, and if you had three thousand five hundred dollars left over you could drill a well of your own, do what the hell you liked and not have to answer to anybody, except the county government in Pioche, a place so far from Rachel that no one was sure it really existed, but from where they kept sending you forms demanding taxes, without offering much in return. But then why should they offer anything to a privileged individual who could afford to live in the desert?

Take Interstate 15 north, then US 93 north, then turn west onto a ninety-two-mile ribbon of asphalt. That's how you get to Rachel.

When Homer traveled along it, the ribbon of asphalt that links Hiko to Warm Springs had the nondescript name of State Highway 375. But a few years later, as a result of an amazing story that a gigantic intergalactic airport disguised as a military base was operating in the area, the road acquired its present title: the 'Extraterrestrial Highway'.

It was Governor Bob Miller who dedicated State Highway 375 to the extraterrestrials. On April 18th 1996 an official ceremony was held in Rachel to celebrate the event and, in his impassioned opening speech, the governor said that, should any extraterrestrials care to visit Nevada's greatest tourist attractions, in particular Las Vegas, they could rest assured that their astrocash and intergalactic plastic would be accepted in all casinos.

When a well-known film company saw the event as a golden opportunity to launch some new footage of an alien invasion, a group of ufologists who had settled in Rachel protested vigorously, considering the venture a threat to their mission of establishing peaceful contact with beings from outer space. Their protests fell on deaf ears, however, and the tourist office announced a new incentive package called the 'E.T. Experience', aimed at promoting excursions into the area around Rachel. Anyone interested in experiencing the thrill of a trip around the alien desert can get further information by calling the Nevada Commission on Tourism on 1-800-NEVADA-8. It's a toll-free number, so it won't cost you anything. But be careful how you use the name of the road, because it's copyrighted The State of Nevada, 1996. All rights reserved; it even says so on the highway signs.

It was thanks to the lights that, not long after the closure of the mine, the town of Rachel found itself reluctantly hauled out of its isolation. Thanks to the lights, and thanks also to a man named Lazarus, who claimed to have worked on an alien spaceship at Papoose Lake, thirty-five miles south of Rachel. He said he had seen no less than nine flying saucers housed in a hangar built into a hillside, where he had been employed by the government to back-engineer the propulsion system of one of these machines, an anti-matter reactor fueled by a copper-orange-colored pellet about the size of a fifty-cent piece.

'Without going into all the technical details, which you're not really interested in and which you wouldn't understand anyway,' said Lazarus unilluminatingly, 'these spacecraft work more or less like an old-fashioned jukebox. You put a coin into a slot and a few seconds later the disc takes off.'

One interviewer asked him if there was any connection between the jukebox mechanism, the birth of rock 'n' roll, and the Fifties boom in sightings of flying saucers. Lazarus replied that while this was a theory worth investigating, as early as 1927 there had already been twelve thousand working jukeboxes scattered across the United States.

'Although I wouldn't rule out the possibility of a link,' he said, 'it seems to me the jukebox is more typical of the Great Depression than of the Fifties. In those days of financial hardship it was a godsend to the managers of bars and restaurants. Just imagine having a whole band of musicians playing for you at the drop of a nickel.'

To give some satisfaction to the interviewer, who was a fan of Elvis Presley, Lazarus added that he had, however, spotted in this underground hangar an alien repairman dressed in a white T-shirt and grease-stained working jeans, with a monkey wrench sticking out of his back pocket. 'He looked a bit like James Dean,' Lazarus mused, 'but his greenish complexion, distinctly receding hairline and insect-like head definitely had something alien about them.'

'So after all the theories we've heard about UFO pilots, do you mean to say they're just the classic little green men?'

'As a scientist I wouldn't express myself in those terms. But yes, that's about the size of it.' Lazarus left a carefully measured pause, then concluded his observations with another platitude. 'Reality isn't as weird as people think, believe you me.'

Lazarus liked to spice his explanations with stories that he made up to give them that extra touch of verisimilitude. At least some skeptics thought he made them up, and that his whole account was a crock of shit from start to finish.

It was thanks to one of these stories that Rachel found its new local resource: lights tourism. Lazarus said that in March or April 1989 he had taken a few friends to the Tibakoo Valley, on the aforementioned State Highway 375, twenty miles south of Rachel, and there they had witnessed what came to be known as the Wednesday tests, lights shooting up into the night sky to perform unusual optical pirouettes, the purpose of which was to test modifications to the UFOs' anti-matter jukeboxes.

After this people with nothing better to think about, people crazy about unknown worlds and bored to tears of disappointment with the known one, would get into their cars every Wednesday and drive down there into the middle of nowhere, in the hope of catching a glimpse of the lights. That was how Rachel came to be the other world's outpost on the planet Earth.

270   Consider now the case of Homer B. Alienson, a man who went nearly twenty years of his life without sleeping because he thought the people around him, including his own mother, were different, that they were body snatchers who wanted to take him over and make him different too. The case of a man who, in order to be able to sleep without being caught by the body snatchers, had no choice but to become, almost inadvertently, a drug addict. This man, who's spent his whole life brutalizing himself in solitude by sniffing heroin, one fine day decides to open up to the world, and leaves his dreary Northwest town, where nobody except the trees and his friend Kurt likes him. He leaves his town and ventures out into the great United States of America in search of love. Now, you might well reply that it is utterly foolish to think you can find love in the great United States of America, where

it's well known that nobody has ever given a damn about anybody else, but we're talking about a coward here, a man guilty of the most abject form of cowardice: emotional apathy. He is a man who has finally decided to respond to the call of the desert – the question of love – and set out on a journey to find a life. It would be a touching story, if the man in question weren't so alienated he hardly exists.

But to come to the point, fate allowed Homer B. Alienson the luxury of reaching Rachel – the luxury of walking mile after mile along a road not served by public transport, a road across a desert where in June a temperature of a hundred and thirteen is nothing out of the ordinary. Fate also granted him the illusion, once he reached Rachel, Nevada, of finding love in a girl called Molly Resident. But since everything has a price, poor Homer paid dearly for the luxury and the illusion.

This is the story of that price.

Well, now.

One day in late June 1991 Homer B. Alienson, from distant Aberdeen, in the State of Washington, arrived on foot in the outskirts of Rachel. He stopped for an instant to contemplate the welcome sign and walked into town.

In the stunning heat of the early afternoon, with the long ribbon of scorching asphalt that was State Highway 375 behind him, Homer's panting, sweaty figure must have made quite an impression on the locals. Homer had nothing about him of the usual lights watcher, who would arrive spruce and dapper, armed with sunglasses, cap, khaki Bermudas and a telephoto lens. He might have been a gunslinger from a long-lost era.

He had no gun, but the way he gripped his baseball betrayed the same mixture of nervousness and composure as a gunslinger ready to draw. He wore no boots, but the way he dragged the rubber soles of his Converses seemed to evoke the jingling of spurs. He had no horse, but then he had no car, either.

Like the gunslingers of the Old West, Homer seemed to be a creature apart, an isolated offshoot of humanity. Like the gunslingers, he appeared in Rachel out of the blue, a loner with no obvious source of income, a man who seemed purpose-built for hiding away and not paying taxes. Like any self-respecting gunslinger, Homer had never let himself get entangled in any permanent emotional relationships, only the occasional platonic attachment: Laura Palmer, the girl from the forbidden planet, Theda Bara, Jackie at the supermarket. In this respect, Homer seemed to be an immature individual, an eternal child who avoided ties and responsibilities. Or perhaps he didn't avoid them. Perhaps he was just afraid of growing up. But in this, too, Homer resembled the old gunslingers, and for this very reason he held a certain fascination for the inhabitants of Rachel and was accepted by them.

They accepted him for what he was, an oddball who walked around in shabby, dirty clothes holding a baseball in his hand, a sort of hero of weakness who one day would meet a waitress in some fast-food joint or a lapdancer, a girl with whom he could have a brief fling, a short-lived affair during which he would not exactly touch, but skim the surface of that different reality which by his nature he could not accept, and once those moments were over he would leave, walking away down that ribbon of asphalt he had come along, while the sunset gilded the desert scrubland and the tumbleweeds bounced on the ground wafted by a hint of a breeze, at the time of day when heat was exhaled from the sandy rocks instead of beating down from the sky and the air filled with night and, in the darkness which before long would envelop everything, scattered lights would appear. Lights that were not mere stars.

*　*　*

There weren't many places to go, in Rachel. There was a convenience store, a sheriff's substation, for the rare occasions when deputies came to settle disputes, a Baptist church, a public library – yes, even here, believe it or not – and a bar. Home Base. Earthlings welcome, said the sign. That was where the lights watchers would stop by, before continuing on their way toward the Tibakoo Valley, toward what they hoped to see.

274 The owner, a Mr McDonald, had made a pile in the mass catering sector and retired to Rachel to open a smaller business and end his brilliant career in a minor key. The fare he offered was cheap, but included some specialties, notably alienburgers. A small, dust-veiled window gave a view of the Nevada sky, furrowed by strips of evanescent cloud that resembled the thoughts of empty-headed cartoon characters; and hanging on the walls were some blurred and dark but nonetheless intriguing photographs; McDonald claimed they were chance snaps of the aliens who took their flying saucers up every Wednesday to test their antimatter reactors by performing ever more unusual pirouettes. There was also a picture by a Flemish painter who specialized in alien portraiture and a shelf with a dozen books that told you all there was to know about the mysterious

and fascinating world of aliens. Lastly, slotted in between the books there was a videocassette with footage of the autopsy carried out on an alien that had been found dead in the desert. No one had ever seen it, because there was no VCR in the bar, but everyone swore the footage was extremely gruesome.

McDonald had never seen a flying saucer in his life, let alone since retiring to Rachel. The same could be said of the other ninety-seven members of the community. But the lights people only needed a single night to see all there was to see. They had their own ideas on the subject, the most ingenious of which was that the inhabitants of Rachel were really aliens in disguise.

Like everybody else, on his arrival in Rachel, Homer headed for McDonald's Home Base, which among other things offered overnight accommodation in a few sinister mobile homes out back. Entering the bar, Homer sat down, put his baseball on the counter and, hardly noticing the photographs, the Flemish painting, the books and all the other things that sent the lights people into ecstasies, fell to contemplating the Nevada sky through the milky veil of the dust-covered window. That transparent rectangle looking out onto nothing made him feel at home, at *his* Home Base.

He ordered an alienburger and asked if there was a free bed for the night.

'When are you thinking of leaving, my friend?' asked McDonald, trying to assess what kind of guy he was dealing with. The plaid logger's shirt and the baseball didn't appeal to him very much.

'Leaving?' Homer echoed him, without taking his eyes off the window. It became immediately clear to both of them that it was going to be a long stay.

In effect he became the ninety-ninth inhabitant of Rachel. He moved into one of the Home Base trailers, and there he remained, giving everyone the impression that this would be his home for quite a while.

He spent most of the day in the bar, sitting on his own at a rickety little table right under the dusty window that looked out onto the desert sky. At one o'clock precisely he would ask McDonald to fry him his usual alienburger, then he would go to the bathroom to systemize himself with heroin. During the afternoon he would fall into a cataleptic state which lasted till sunset.

The people of Rachel soon grew accustomed to his strange but innocuous presence. Homer had about as much impact on the sleepy equilibrium of that small community as an odd-shaped stone might have on the age-old indifference of a remote and rocky landscape.

By some curious coincidence the people of Rachel took to greeting him in the same way as the guy in the Aberdeen post office. They would point a crooked forefinger toward him and say in a hoarse, broken voice: 'Ho-mer.' Then they would smile at him without the slightest malice. He would raise his hand and walk on, head bowed. That was his way of greeting them and going along with the joke. He realized that there was no ill will in their way of pretending he was an alien, indeed that it was a sign of affection, and this helped him not to get uptight, not to start wondering what possible conspiracies might lie behind this remarkable coincidence.

As a matter of fact his features had lost any resemblance they might ever have had to Steven Spielberg's little alien. Now he looked more like Christopher Walken in *The Deer Hunter*. One night when he was out walking in the desert, Homer had lost the beret that Kurt had given him at Van Nuys. He'd replaced it with a red bandanna he'd bought at the store and wore swathed around his forehead, Indian-style.

He also had a revolver now. He'd found it on one of

his trips into the hills around Rachel, where he went searching for Old West relics, as he called them: petroglyphs, arrowheads and other traces of the Paiute Indians who had camped in that area in earlier times.

He knew nothing about Indians, nor was he interested in learning anything about them. He went out on a trip whenever he didn't fancy spending the whole day at McDonald's Home Base. There was no other reason; it was a habit he acquired automatically, a sort of instinctive integration into the landscape, not unlike the relationship he'd had with the trees in the woods around Aberdeen.

One day he returned from a trip with a sand-encrusted, rusty old gun.

'It looks like a Peacemaker,' said McDonald when Homer showed it to him.

Homer raised his eyebrows.

'A Colt forty-five. Pat Garrett used one to kill Billy the Kid. It'd make a nice museum piece if it wasn't so battered.'

'I'll clean it up,' Homer decided.

'Clean it up? What the hell for?'

'A gun can always come in handy.'

'One that works, maybe. All you could do with that bit of old scrap iron is hit someone on the head.'

'I'll clean it up,' repeated Homer with immovable conviction.

'What about ammunition? What use is a gun without ammunition?'

'I'll find that too, sooner or later,' replied Homer, taking back his gun.

'In the hills?'

'In the hills,' Homer confirmed.

He spent weeks repairing the Peacemaker. He would eat his alienburger, systemize himself with heroin and spend the whole day fiddling with the gun. He'd rub it, sand it, blow on it, peer down the barrel, polish it, take it apart, clean it piece by piece, grease it, put it back together again, and finally lay it on the rickety table, next to the baseball, to assess how his work was progressing.

'Wow, Homer. You've done a really good job. A heck of a good job,' McDonald congratulated him one day. 'I never thought you'd manage it. It's a real nice gun.'

'I've cleaned it up,' said Homer without taking his eyes off the gun.

'Now we've got to solve the ammunition problem.'

'Yeah,' said Homer. He glanced at the sky through the dust-veiled window and added: 'I'll take a walk in the hills tomorrow.'

McDonald said: 'Good luck.'

'Thanks,' said Homer, with some feeling.

The next day, when he returned from his trip, Homer showed McDonald what he'd found. An old ammunition box bearing the words 30 CARTRIDGES CALIBER 44. WINCHESTER MODEL 1873 RIFLE.

'Shit, Homer. Another museum piece. Must be at least a hundred years old. You sure do find things up there.'

'I could put them in my gun,' said Homer hopefully.

'I'm afraid not, pal. Even if they're still usable, they're the wrong caliber. You have a Colt forty-five and these are forty-fours. They're for a Winchester. It says so here, look.'

Homer frowned. Then he stretched out his hand and said: 'I'll keep them anyway. You never know.'

'Sure, Homer. Are you going for another trip into the hills tomorrow?'

'I don't know.'

'Wonder what you'll find next.'

'A rifle, that's what I'd like. One to go with this ammunition.'

'That's pretty unlikely, Homer.'

'You never know, Mac.'

* * *

A whole summer passed, then a fall, then a winter too. Sometimes it rained, turning the sandy terrain of the desert valley into a quagmire. Homer alternated days of catatonic meditation at the rickety table under the dusty window with days of walking in the hills, among the abandoned mines and the old Indian camps. Usually he came back empty-handed, but some evenings he produced some unexpected museum pieces, as McDonald called them. He found an Indian tomahawk, a pickax, a boot complete with spur, and a photograph of a prostitute from the days of the saloons, but not the rifle he craved.

'Never mind,' McDonald would console him. 'You could open an Old West museum with all the stuff you've found.'

Homer didn't reply, but it was clear from his expression that the idea of opening a museum left him cold. It was the rifle he was after. Or, alternatively, a box of bullets for his Peacemaker.

'Listen, you could *buy* a rifle. I've got to go to Pioche next week. Why don't you come with me? There's a good gunstore there. You could buy a brand-new rifle, with ammunition and everything,' McDonald suggested.

Homer's face again expressed total indifference. The rifle must be one that was linked to the history of the place; it was all part of the process of integrating into the landscape. It was one of his pointless fixations. McDonald had got to know Homer by now, so he didn't press him. When he tried to give him advice it was more for the sake of making conversation than in any real hope of convincing him.

Besides, Homer was proving to be something of an attraction for McDonald's bar. He had an incredible, fascinating story to tell, the story of a guy surrounded by alien presences who hadn't slept for twenty years for fear that they would take him over and make him different; of his discovery that his mother was no longer his mother, though outwardly she seemed the same as ever; of his meeting with a boy who lived under the North Aberdeen Bridge and caught poisoned fish in the river Wishkah; of his integration into a system more wonderful than the world of the Wizard of Oz, a system that could protect people from difference and give them a new perspective on things, an ecstatic indifference to the trivial concerns of everyday life; and of the cognitive experience of the world through the catatonic contemplation of TV.

It sounded pretty far-fetched, and McDonald didn't believe a word of it. But it would be like manna from heaven to the lights people. It was the kind of thing they lapped up. McDonald could already imagine them, those gullible fools hanging on the every word of this lunatic dressed in his red bandanna and his plaid shirt, as he recounted in exhaustive detail how he'd given up sleeping after seeing some stupid science-fiction movie, or footage of hypothetical, extraordinary, not-scientifically-attested events, as Homer called it. People would come from all over America to listen to Homer's incredible story, and maybe even from Europe, once word got around. It couldn't fail.

'Listen, Homer,' McDonald said one day, 'it's not healthy to keep things bottled up. You brood too much. You've got to open up a little.'

Homer waited to hear what McDonald was driving at.

'I'm talking about your story. Your not sleeping for twenty years and stuff. You need to talk about it to somebody.'

'I don't understand, Mac,' said Homer, puzzled. 'I've already told you all there is to tell. I haven't kept anything back, I assure you. I even offered to integrate you into the system once, but you didn't want to know. Have you changed your mind, Mac? Do you want to systemize yourself?' and he held out his baseball to him.

'Forget your damned ball. That's not what I meant. I wasn't referring to myself. Don't you understand?'

'No.'

McDonald took a chair and placed it by the rickety table. He sat down and tried to look Homer in the eyes, which wasn't easy. Homer's gaze was vacant, like that of a fish in its bowl.

'I'd like you to tell your story to the people who come to Rachel to see the lights.'

'Why the hell should I do that?'

'Because they know about such things. Weird stories. Aliens, spaceships.'

Homer said nothing.

'They'll understand you. They might be able to give you some advice.'

Homer remained silent.

'You mustn't be put off by their appearance. They look like fools, I know, and some of them are. But they spend their lives studying these phenomena.'

Homer grimaced.

'Where's the harm in trying? At least you'll have had a chat with someone. It certainly won't do you any harm. You never talk to anyone. You sit at this table all day long and nobody knows what the hell you're thinking about.'

'*I* know what I'm thinking about, Mac.'

'Don't take me literally, for Christ's sake. It was a figure of speech.'

'Okay.'

'You never know what a good, healthy conversation might lead to.'

'That's just it, I don't know. What good can possibly come of talking about my private life to strangers?'

'Who knows? Maybe it'd help you get your ideas straight. Maybe someone could give you a tip about how to find this love from another world. Because one thing's for sure, Homer, you're not going to find it in those hills you're always exploring.'

Homer lowered his eyes and stared at the surface of the rickety table. McDonald put his hand on Homer's shoulder and said, earnestly: 'What have you got to lose, Homer?'

'I don't go up to people I don't know and start talking to them.'

'You don't have to go up to anyone. I'll see to that. The people come in, I fix them something to eat, give them some information, warm up the atmosphere, then, you know how it is, one thing leads to another and I get around to it, in the most natural way in the world. Things take care of themselves if you let them run their own course. You won't have to do anything. You can sit here at your table and think about whatever you like; or clean your gun, if that's what you'd rather do. They'll come over to you. They'll bombard you with questions, you'll see. All you have to do is answer them.'

And that was exactly what happened. The lights people would arrive with their credulous expressions and their photographic equipment. McDonald would draw them in with his easy manner and divert them to Homer's table, where Homer would somehow find himself telling his story to a set of perfect strangers.

McDonald had been right: the lights watchers were crazy about Homer, his story and his monkish air, this burned-out survivor who dispensed wisdom in chunks of absurdity. Soon they forgot all about the lights and the great intergalactic airport. After all it was just another top-secret military base – slightly larger than average, admittedly, but otherwise nothing out of the ordinary. Now they came to McDonald's bar to see Homer and hear him talk, and instead of telephoto lenses they brought Dictaphones.

One of them, however, made the mistake of asking if he could photograph him. Homer said no and flew into a rage. The tourist was very alarmed and McDonald intervened.

'I only wanted to take a photo of him,' the guy explained.

'What's got into you, Homer? Why don't you want to be photographed?' asked McDonald.

'You know why.'

'No, I don't. How the hell could I?'

'When someone takes a photograph of you, your body burns up and when you're dead your soul lives on, imprisoned in the photograph.'

'For Pete's sake, Homer. That's just Indian nonsense. What does it matter to you? What do *you* know about Indian beliefs?'

'I know plenty.'

'Plenty? Why, only a short while ago you were wandering around in the forests of the Northwest like some logger. Now you find a couple of arrowheads and a tomahawk and you think you know everything about Indians.'

'Not everything, but plenty. And you're forgetting about the photograph.' Homer was referring to the photograph of a young Indian couple that he'd found in the hills. They looked very much in love and Homer had burned it to set their souls free so that they could rest in peace forever.

'Okay. But so what?' snorted McDonald. 'Like I said: what do you care about a stupid Indian superstition about photography?'

'Enough not to want to be photographed.'

McDonald raised his eyes to the ceiling. The tourist looked bewildered.

'It's no good arguing, Mac. You know that when I say no, I mean no.' That was true. McDonald knew how stubborn Homer could be. He was a gentle, even like-able nutcase in some respects, but when he got his back up it was better to let him be. So McDonald looked at the lights watcher as if to say he'd better drop the idea of the photograph.

The tourist, only too glad to take the hint, dashed out of the bar. McDonald turned toward Homer and looked at him with the air of one who expects at least a few words of apology.

'I'm sorry, Mac. But that's the way it is,' said Homer, firmly. 'I don't mind telling my story, but I won't be photographed.'

McDonald thought it over. At length he said, 'Okay, okay. Whatever you say. No photographs.' Homer had become Rachel's main attraction. And he was a gold mine for Home Base. There was no point in ruining everything over a stupid photograph. Besides, this whim of Homer's might enhance his aura of mystery. That would whet the tourists' appetites even more.

'No photographs,' McDonald reassured him again.

It became a kind of job, and the relationship between Homer and McDonald was regulated by a tacit agreement, a contract whose terms, though never explicitly stated, were clear to both parties.

Homer got full board and lodging in exchange for his presence in McDonald's bar from nine to twelve in the morning and from six to ten in the evening. He had two days off a week, during which he could go on his trips. They were pretty good terms: all expenses paid for telling the story of his life. Jobs like that aren't easy to come by.

Yet Homer wasn't happy. Not that he ever had been happy, of course, but although a tendency to be depressed was part of his nature, having to tell the story of his life every day made it worse. It got to the point where he no longer even recognized himself. He listened to himself reminiscing to the lights people about his childhood, lingering over every sad little detail, and he felt as if that childhood had never belonged to him. Everything he'd always thought important faded into insignificance. The more he talked about himself, the less sure he was of his own identity. He felt like he had when Kurt had kept calling him Boddah.

He wasn't himself. Not just figuratively speaking. He really wasn't himself. Sometimes he thought he had nothing to complain about and that he was just a pathetic, childish whiner. For too long he'd been totally indifferent to his own life and to the words he used to describe it to people he didn't know, people he saw as a single, insignificant, faceless individual. It was hard not to complain. It was hard to bear the weight of his new celebrity. For in a sense he had become famous, a public figure. People came from all over America to listen to him, as if he were some kind of rock star. The lights would go out and the frenzied crowd would stamp and cheer and he would be standing up there, deceiving his audience. He felt he was duping those adoring people by telling them incredible stories, making them believe things he no longer even believed himself. Sometimes he felt as if McDonald made him punch a time clock before he went on stage. And he had tried – God, how he had tried. Apparently he hadn't tried hard enough, since he couldn't bring himself to love what he had become. But when he reflected on the fact that he had moved and astonished masses of people with his words, he was gratified. Then he would think he was one of those narcissists who only appreciate things when they are gone. He was too sensitive, that was his problem. Which was strange in one who had tried not to have any feelings, who dreaded feelings. Apart from systemic ones, of course. What wouldn't he have given to regain the enthusiasm he'd had in his childhood, before his mother had given him that piece of coal for Christmas. He still couldn't get over the frustration, the guilt, the empathy he felt for others. There was some good in everyone, and maybe he loved people too much, even the different ones. He loved them so much that he kept aloof from them, sheltering in his irremediable sadness. How stupid, sad, insensitive, ungrateful he was. Hell, why couldn't he just enjoy life? He used to imagine that he would meet a love from another world one day, a goddess in human form who would be the cynosure of all men's eyes. He no longer cared even about her. Or about the child that she might have given him. A baby girl, a daughter who would have reminded him of everything he had once been. Full of joy and love, the child would have kissed everyone she met, for the world would have seemed good to her and nobody would have harmed her. When he saw that vision, Homer would grow frightened and delirious. He couldn't bear the thought that one day his daughter might become unhappy and self-destructive, that she would flirt with death as he was doing. He had all he needed and he thanked the Lord for that, but it wasn't true that he loved people. He had loved them in the past, up to age seven. From that time on he had loathed the human race. Or rather, he had loved people and loathed the human race. It seemed so easy for people to get along and have compassion: that was what made him so fucking sad. He saw their destiny and felt sorry for them.

He thanked everyone, from the bottom of his burning, nauseous stomach. He thanked them for traveling all that way just to listen to his stupid story. He was too erratic, too moody. He no longer felt the slightest passion. Often he looked at the Peacemaker he'd found in the desert, regretting that he still hadn't found any ammunition for it, and a new idea started to grow in him: that it was better to burn out than fade away. Than be switched off in a small way every day of our lives, like the living-room light that we put out each evening before we sleep.

Before we sleep.

* * *

Matters were further complicated by an unexpected event.

Not unexpected in the true sense of the word. Unexpected in the sense that Homer wasn't expecting it.

It was an event that can be summed up in a few words.

One day, Homer went into the bathroom in Home Base to systemize himself with heroin as usual. He removed the dowel from the baseball, stuck his finger in the hole and found nothing. He looked inside and saw nothing. He shook the ball and heard nothing; no familiar rattle of a baggie. He rushed out of the bathroom, went over to the counter and asked McDonald to lend him a knife.

'What do you want with a knife in the bathroom?' McDonald asked. Homer went back in there without replying. He sliced open the baseball and saw what he didn't want to see. There was no more heroin.

He paced to and fro in the six square feet of the bathroom. He kicked the door. He panicked. He sobbed. He couldn't breathe. He rested his back against the wall and slid down to the floor, as people do at particularly dramatic moments on TV or at the movie theater.

He had never been to a movie theater.

There was no more heroin.
There was no more heroin.
There was no more heroine.

People think the desert is just a desert, but it's full of animals. Rats, snakes, rattlesnakes, giant wasps, hornets, bats, desert toads, horned toads, desert tortoises, digger owls, rabbits that keep their ears erect to disperse the heat, skunks, raccoons, dwarf foxes and, of course, him, the Coyote, always hungry, always out there somewhere, invisible.

People think there's no water in the desert, and indeed there isn't. But some desert animals dig deep down till they find a layer of wet sand.

Whether there's any heroin in the desert is not a question that most people have ever thought about. But what if someone did happen to think about it? If you think about such things it's because you need them, and if you find yourself needing them you'd better start saying your prayers, because you're never going to find them in the desert. Whatever illusions you may have had on the subject

* * *

A psychiatrist who had decided to try to discover the mysterious mechanism that caused people to become drug addicts put the following question to a distinguished gentleman who had been around the system most of his life: 'Why do you believe you can't do without heroin?'

'Believe?' said the distinguished gentleman, who was getting on in years by this time. 'I don't believe anything, doctor. I simply need it, in order to stay alive.'

You have to give these people the answers they deserve. I don't believe anything, Mr Psychiatric Social Worker. That's the way to talk to them.

Believe. Like hell I believe. I've never believed a fucking thing all my life. That's why people become drug addicts, because they don't believe, didn't anybody ever tell you that? I don't *believe* I'm dying, I *am* dying.

As for the idea that I *just* have to be strong, because it's only withdrawal that makes me feel like I'm dead, allow me to say, Mr Psychiatric Worker, that withdrawal is a totality, and that I'm not merely weak, I've attracted onto myself all the weakness in the universe. I don't just *feel* weak, I *am* weakness. Weakness in all its cosmic enervation. How can a quintessence of weakness even try to imagine it's strong? I assure you it's not that I don't want to – if it were just a question of dying, I'd die. A quick, painless death. A gunshot in the mouth, for example. I'd settle for that any day, believe me. But the point here is different, very different. The point is that I could die because of the very fact that I'm alive.

While acknowledging the considerable discomfort that an individual may feel when suddenly deprived of heroin, doctors categorically deny that withdrawal is ever actually life-threatening.

'There are a number of products that can help in such cases,' one of them added. 'Such as clonidine, which has long been used in detoxification from opiates and in particular in treatments involving the subsequent use of naltrexone, though I must confess that, because it's an $alpha_2$-adrenergenic, it often causes hypotension.'

Okay, but what does a patient do if he happens to be in the middle of a tract of desert scrubland in Nevada?

'I fear that failing an adequate support therapy, he would simply have to put up with the withdrawal symptoms for a while.'

And what might they be?

'Insomnia, watery eyes, muscular spasms and pains, stomach cramps, hyperventilation, hypothermia, pains in the ligaments, vomiting and diarrhea. Those are the symptoms that manifest themselves twelve hours after the final dose, and they can continue for up to five or six days. Plus a few other more trivial problems such as goosebumps, dilated pupils, frequent yawning, chills alternating with hot flushes, and an inability to concentrate. As well as anxiety, a deep sense of insecurity, an inability to face up to situations, and a certain degree of hostility toward the surrounding environment.'

Five or six days, you say.

'Let's say that after six days the first phase of the withdrawal syndrome will be over. At the end of that phase, from a chemical point of view, the heroin addict can be described as virtually detoxed.'

Only virtually?

'Yes, because on the sixth day a second phase begins, during which you suffer from low blood pressure, dilated pupils, metabolic dysfunctions and a general state of physical fatigue and psychological depression.'

And how long does that phase last?

'Several months. Usually about six.'

Shit, that must be pretty tough.

'As I said, the detox is virtual. Without the appropriate support therapy an addict is unlikely to hold out for more than a month after the beginning of the second phase before he reverts to taking heroin.'

What if the subject has no support and no access to heroin?

'It depends. But it's highly likely that self-destructive urges will emerge. During the second phase of the withdrawal syndrome the addict is a kind of chronic misfit; someone who just can't handle life. He starts getting delusions, thinking that the whole world is, how can I put it. . .'

Fucked up.

'Something like that.'

Now he was in his trailer, his head swathed by the red bandanna. He was too weak to get out of bed. He was too exhausted to imagine any kind of movement and too restless and desperate to bear lying there motionless like that. Whatever he tried to do was unbearable – moving, keeping still, turning over. The heat was infernal but he wished he had a blanket to wrap around him because he was shivering. He had begun to sweat. He was so tired he wanted to sleep, so weary he just didn't care about the body snatchers anymore, but he couldn't keep his eyes closed because they beat against his eyelids and when he kept them open he couldn't stand the dim light that filtered through a desolating little curtain. His nose was encrusted with snot and there were times when he felt like he was suffocating and he tried to breathe with his mouth open like a fish in its bowl, but however hard he tried he didn't seem to be able to get an ounce of oxygen out of that shoebox of a trailer. Sometimes, in the interminable moments of suffocation, he had flash-backs of things he'd seen from the windows of the many buses that had brought him there: the rusty wreckage of a pickup protruding from the dry scrub of an untended garden; a shadowy veranda in the hot sun of the early afternoon; an abandoned gas station; a tire hanging from the branch of a tree like a swing. Some of these images seemed to have the power to relax him, but as soon as he almost began breathing again those same images would rend his soul and he would start to cry. He should have asked himself why the fuck he'd traveled all that way, but he didn't have the strength to ask any questions, let alone search for answers among memories he didn't seem to have. Besides, he couldn't care less why he'd come down there. He'd be perfectly happy to spend the few days that were left to him stretched out on his bed, in his trailer, in back of Home Base.

*　　*　　*

It is written that when they came to the place called Golgotha, which means the place of the Skull, they gave Him wine mixed with gall, but having tasted it He would not drink.

Now, since it is well known that opium mixed with wine has a distinctly bitter taste, scriptural scholars believe that the gall was in fact opium, which was offered to Him to alleviate the pain of the crucifixion, and that He refused the drink because the Spirit that had previously led Him into the desert, so that He could be tempted by the Devil, was in fact opium.

Hours of seemingly endless discomfort gave way to the evening twilight. The trailer door opened and Homer withdrew, turtle-like, into a shell of absolute stillness, waiting. A silhouette entered the darkness. The silence in the trailer was complete. The silhouette came a few steps forward through the darkness, sat down on the edge of the bed and shook Homer's shoulder with its hand.

'Are you asleep?' said the silhouette, which spoke with the voice of a young woman. Homer remained motionless in his shell. That's the way to survive in the desert, by lying flat and still. Estivation. The desert toad digs a hole five feet deep and spends fifty weeks a year in it without food or water. Rodents dig holes. Even *owls* dig holes, just to survive.

The silhouette brushed his forehead with the back of its hand to feel if it was warm. Homer was sweating, as he had been all day. On the hottest days you can sweat nineteen pints, in those parts. Only you don't realize you're sweating so much, because the heat is so great that the drops of sweat evaporate instantly. A heroin addict in withdrawal can sweat as much as a human being in the desert.

The silhouette in the darkness bent down and put its lips to Homer's ear. How much can a heroin addict in withdrawal in the desert sweat, when an unknown girl is about to whisper something to him in the dark? 'You'll have to move over a bit. This is my bed too for tonight.' Nineteen pints. He sweats nineteen pints. It isn't humanly possible to sweat more. 'You'll feel better tomorrow, you'll see.' What about inhumanly? How much is it possible to sweat, inhumanly speaking? He heard the rustle of the dark silhouette taking off an item of clothing. He felt the silhouette's eyes rest on him. If only he could systemize himself a bit. One grain of system would be enough. One drop of heroin. Give drink to a thirsty man. There have been years when not a single drop of rain has fallen in the whole of Death Valley. He contrived to make room for her. He turned on his side and made room for her, pretending to turn over in his sleep. Death Valley is in California. He was in Nevada. He heard the dark silhouette of the girl lie down beside him. Plants cope with the lack of water by adapting to Liebig's law. They halve their proportions, shrivel their leaves. They regress. He heard the dark silhouette of the girl breathing. The heroin addict copes with the lack of heroin by halving his proportions, by shriveling into himself. He regresses toward the enchantment of childhood and his childish fears become the desperation of an adult who's scared of everything, even of a dark silhouette that lies down beside him in the darkness of a trailer. In Rachel, Nevada.

Where did I go?

Next day, when McDonald came to ask what he wanted to eat, the darkly lit girl was no longer there. Nor was the darkness. The dim light that filtered through the small curtain blinded him. Homer imagined the dazzling glare of a high summer's day in the desert.

'Is it hot today?' he asked McDonald.

'Can't you tell?'

'No, I can't. It's hot but I feel almost cold.'

'You'll get over it, don't worry.'

'I'm not so sure about that.'

'Do you want your usual hamburger?'

'Yeah.'

'Don't you think you ought to eat something else? Something more appropriate to your condition? A salad, maybe.'

'No.'

McDonald didn't press him. 'All right,' he said and made as if to leave.

'Mac.'

Mac turned. 'Yes?'

'Someone slept here with me last night.'

'I know.'

'Who was it?'

'A girl from out of town.'

'A girl?'

'Yeah.'

'Why did she sleep with me?'

'I didn't have a free trailer, so I thought I'd. . .'

Homer said nothing.

'It won't happen again. I've already found her a place to stay.'

'Stay?'

McDonald hesitated. 'Yeah. She'll be staying here for a while.'

'Here in Rachel?'

'Yeah.'

'What's she going to be doing here?'

'Working in the bar.' He said it as if it were a weight off his mind.

'In the bar?'

'In the bar.'

'At Home Base?'

'Listen, Homer, you've been in this state for quite a while. You lie here sick, the lights people come to the bar, they don't find you, they're disappointed and they leave. I thought I'd offer an alternative attraction.'

Homer said nothing.

'You know how it is, she's pretty. Real pretty.'

'. . .'

'Molly. Molly Resident.' He shook his head and added: 'My God, she's gorgeous. She's got something. . .' He paused, searching for the right word. '. . .special. Special, yeah. You should see those stupid tourists. They drool over her, but they're too dumb to try anything.' He sighed. 'If only I were a few years younger.'

'So the bottom line is, you've given her my job,' said Homer bitterly.

'Try to see it my way, Homer. I couldn't let the whole bar go to pot. Besides, you didn't seem to like entertaining the tourists with your story.'

'No, it pissed me off,' replied Homer bluntly.

'You're not offended, are you?'

'No.'

'You can stay here as long as you like. The important thing is that you get better soon.'

'What kind of stories do you get *her* to tell them?'

'It's not the way you think. She's a professional. She serves at the tables.'

'There are two tables in the bar.'

'Plus the counter.'

'Oh, sure, the counter.'

'I told you, she's a professional. She has a way with her, she's got this special walk and a certain style.'

'A certain style.'

'They drool over her, I'm telling you.'

'. . .'

'Well, I've got to get back to the bar. I'll bring you your hamburger, then.'

'. . .'

'See you later, Homer,' said McDonald, and again made as if to leave.

'Mac.'

'Yeah?'

'One more thing, Mac.'

'What is it, Homer?'

'There's one thing I don't understand. I don't understand what a waitress who's suddenly materialized out of nowhere has to do with Home Base. Why on earth should the lights people be so interested in an ordinary girl? They don't come to Rachel for the girls.'

'She's not an ordinary girl, Homer.'

'Yeah, I know. The walk, the certain style. But she can never be more than a pretty girl.'

'Sure she can.'

'How? What's she got to do with the lights and the stories about aliens?'

'There's something I haven't told you, Homer,' said McDonald in a funereal tone.

Homer waited for him to go on.

'You see, the lights people think she's your love from another world. They think she's come all the way from outer space for your sake. That's why nobody dares to try anything with her.'

Homer felt his head spinning. 'And does she really come from outer space?'

'What the hell are you talking about, Homer? Of course she doesn't. She's from Las Vegas.'

'Then where did the lights people get the idea...'
McDonald didn't give him time to finish.

'It was me. I spread the rumor and now everyone thinks she's your love from another world.'

Homer froze.

'I did it for the sake of Home Base. I hope you understand.'

But Homer's expression did not show understanding.

Later McDonald brought him his usual alienburger. Barely a quarter of an hour had passed before Homer threw it up.

You think your life has been spent in too confined a space. A small town of a few thousand inhabitants, a house so nondescript you hardly even recognize it when you go home, a television with its worldwide news. The same thoughts day after day, and a coat of grayness over everything, so uniform it might have been spray-painted on. So you think that you might be able to escape by leaving home, that you can open up to the external world, expand and give a meaning to the fact that you are still to some extent alive, a meaning that is not a real meaning but merely something unexpected, something extraneous to the geometry of confined spaces. An encounter, perhaps. A girl who smiles at you as if she'd just been born. Then you ask yourself why such an event should be so powerful as to change your life and the answer is, no, it doesn't change it at all. And even if it did, the change would be merely a question of density: the same confined space, but with the addition of a person who instead of smiling at you as if she'd just been born glares at you resentfully. But you also think that it doesn't have to be so, that there is no universal law that all meetings have to end in the same way. And even if there were, why worry about how it's going to end, when things and love affairs do that of their own accord? End, that is. So you think that in any case it's worth leaving home. Worth seeing where it takes you.

Now, while you're having these thoughts you don't imagine for one moment that your baseball, the object in which you have placed your soul – what for you *is* your soul – might revert to being what it was before, an empty leather sphere. Nor do you imagine that, after losing the most vital thing you had in the world, you might find yourself in the middle of the desert, lying on your bed in a mobile home, wearing a red bandanna and a plaid flannel shirt. Nor do you imagine that the only thing that could give a meaning to all this might be your falling in love with a girl you've never seen. It doesn't occur to you that the situation is quite absurd and that you really ought to be thinking about something else, like having someone take you to a doctor, since you're more dead than alive, or finding some way of ending it all, since you wish you were rather dead than alive.

But the most incredible thing is not what you might think, nor the idiotic idea that all you have to do to avoid losing your soul is put it in a baseball, nor the fact of falling in love with a still faceless girl. No. The most incredible thing, the thing you find quite unaccountable, is how quickly all this comes to seem to you the most natural thing in the world.

After all, how many days had passed since he had woken up in this state? Two? Three? A week? A month? Certainly not more than a month, maybe even less. Much less. And yet it was like he'd been born in that mobile home and had never left it. To Homer, who had grown up in a land of rainy days and gray skies, it seemed like he had only ever known the dazzling daily routine of the heat that filtered through the desolating little curtain of the even more desolating dusty window that gave onto the backyard of Home Base, where the only significant thing to look at was three crates of beer stacked one on top of the other.

Even more incredible was the fact that nothing of what had existed in the past mattered at all. The differents, the film of the body snatchers, the many years of forced sleeplessness, the space toys, the nostalgia geeks, Kurt, the system. These were all things he remembered perfectly well but which he couldn't place correctly in his life. They were things that came to mind, like the lines of certain poems he had learned by heart in his schooldays. Of course, all this could be simply put down to his deplorable error of mistaking a bit of heroin for his soul, for his whole life. It might be argued that Homer himself was responsible for reducing his soul to powder, a white powder that he sniffed through his nose so that it would go down into his lungs, from his lungs to his blood, and with his blood around and about his body. But did that change anything? He had grown accustomed to the routine of the mobile home because he felt that the choice had not been his, for adapting is not always a choice. Sometimes it is an instinct of survival, the instinct whereby everyone grows accustomed to everything, an instinct to which junkies are particularly prone, given their propensity for bad habits. He had grown accustomed to it because, once he had reached that point, leaving Rachel and returning to his world was something extraneous to his imagination. He lived for the evening twilight now, when he imagined that the door might open and that she might appear in the doorway, Molly Resident, the girl he had never seen but whom everyone saw as his love from another world, the person for whom he had traveled so far and had reduced himself to the state he was in. He would imagine her standing in the doorway asking if she could come in, telling him she had thought she would bring him something to eat, and he would sit up, eat what she had given him and by some miracle manage not to vomit. Then she would ask him if he would like to go for a walk in the desert, by night, now that it was cooler, because it would be good for him to walk a little. He would pretend to be undecided, then he would accept her invitation and go out with her into the desert by night, in the hope that something romantic would happen, that she would say some-thing intimate or that he would find the courage to lift his hand and run his fingers through her darkly lit hair.

But the routine of the trailer did not include any of this and the days passed with him feeling worse than before. And when evening fell and it was clear that she was not going to come, Homer would try to remember the details of that night when she had slept in the trailer with him. To tell the truth there weren't many such details – only her back, at which he had tried to take a peek now and then, and the anguished way he had lain there all night measuring the rhythm of that back as it breathed under a white T-shirt. He would lie there, reliving the details of that night that he still remembered, till the sun rose, and he was alone with the discomfort that never left him, with the dazzling heat of the desert that filtered through the small curtain and with the time that lay between him and the following evening.

Predictably, his longing to see her continued to grow. He told himself that this was because he had not been able to see her. He consoled himself with the thought that perhaps she was nothing special. Not all that attractive, perhaps even plain. But he knew this wasn't true. If McDonald had told him she was gorgeous, she really must be. McDonald would never have given the role of his love from another world to an ordinary girl.

He knew nothing about her except her name, Molly Resident. But he could imagine her. She must be as lonely as he was, a girl nobody understood. The pain of not being able to meet her was almost as acute as his stomach ache, his lack of heroin and the resulting symptoms. Almost.

If only he could see her just once, for a few seconds. That was all he wanted. Of course, he could have done the easiest and most sensible thing in the world: tell McDonald that he wanted to meet her. He had a perfect right – she was his creation, after all. Wasn't she one of the stars of his story? Wasn't that why she was there in the first place, to be his love from another world? But irrefutable as these arguments seemed, he couldn't bring himself to raise the subject with McDonald.

He didn't want to make the first move. It was a question of pride, of principle. McDonald had ditched Homer at the first sign of trouble. He hadn't thought twice about it. He'd replaced him on the spot, immediately started looking around for a new attraction for his third-rate watering hole.

But it wasn't just that. If it had only been a matter of pride, he would certainly have spoken to McDonald. Pride, as everyone knows, is not a drug addict's strong point. No, there was another, even more important fact: McDonald did his level best to keep Homer away from the girl. Homer never saw any concrete evidence, but he was paranoid that he was being treated like a leper who had to be kept away from the bar and its new attraction at all costs. In the state he was in, he wouldn't have been a pleasant sight for the customers. Besides, it was only too obvious that McDonald regarded Homer as a loose cannon, who was likely to cause disaster at any moment. He might blurt out to the tourists that Molly Resident wasn't really the love from another world that he was looking for; he might let slip that it was all just a gimmick McDonald had thought up to keep people coming to Rachel. Or he might fall in love with the girl and run away with her, leaving McDonald in the shit, with no attractions to offer his customers.

The more he thought about it the clearer it seemed to him that McDonald had every interest in keeping him away from the bar. He even began to suspect he was planning to kill him. With Homer dead, no one would ever discover the deception. Molly Resident would be able to stay on at Home Base, as the inconsolable widow from another world. Then, in a few months' time, everyone would have forgotten Homer, and Molly might begin to accept some consolation – from McDonald. He was clearly only too ready to provide it. It was obvious he liked her. She's gorgeous, he'd said. And he'd also said, If only I were a few years younger. That's what he'd said. His very words. He was bound to start pawing at her sooner or later. He was dying to do so, and who was to say he hadn't already.

He felt the blood rise to his head. Shit, he'd like to split the guy's fucking head open. He'd have done it, too, if only he'd been feeling stronger. With his genuine Indian tomahawk, fuck it.

He stopped eating his meals. If he wanted to recover, he couldn't run the risk of McDonald poisoning him. He had a strong suspicion he was trying to. Fasting couldn't make him feel worse than he did already, and he brought up everything he ate, as it was.

It did make him feel worse. In two days he got so weak he didn't even have the strength to turn on his side. All he felt capable of was waiting for death. He could already see it from a distance, in a kind of backward tracking shot looking down from his soul as it left his body. The heart-rending background music grew louder. The picture cut to the trailer window, to the desolating little curtain stirred by an artificial wind, then there was an aerial panning shot of the desert, where the mobile homes of Rachel were reduced to little white dots on the dusty wasteland. But just as he was expecting the final credits to scroll down, he heard a noise outside the trailer. Footsteps moving in the backyard of Home Base, someone taking bottles of beer from the stack of crates. The sound revived him. It's her, he thought. They're running out of bottles in the bar and McDonald has told her to replenish the fridge, he thought. Had he not been dying he would have been able to sit up and peek at her from behind the curtain. How beautiful she was. She was so beautiful that the sight of her wrung all the breath from his lungs. He saw her take the bottles in one hand and cradle them against her chest with her arm. The bottles delicately crushed her breasts, she turned about and walked unsteadily up the steps to the back door, her figure passed from the dazzling sunlight into the crack of darkness left by the open door, and she became part of the darkness, until he could no longer see her. She was so beautiful, it was as if she had conceived herself, personally selecting her favorite features, the forms she considered most desirable, the gentlest and most sensual way of moving her body. She seemed newly landed from another planet, a more highly evolved world than ours where imperfections belonged to the realms of prehistory.

Molly from another world.

On the morning of the third day of his fast, McDonald came to see him. 'You must eat something, Homer.'

Homer shook his head.

'Maybe we'd better call a doctor.'

Again Homer shook his head. His breathing was wheezy, his eyes brimmed with tears.

'Are you sure? I could take you to hospital in the pickup, if you'd rather.'

Homer gazed at McDonald imploringly. 'Please,' he said in a faint voice.

'What?'

'Let me see her.'

McDonald pretended not to understand. 'What are you talking about?'

'I'm dying, Mac.'

'Don't be stupid.'

'I'm dying, Mac. Let me see her, please. Just once. Please, Mac.'

McDonald looked around in embarrassment, hands on hips. He sighed and said: 'You just rest, now.' Then he left, without another word.

In the end McDonald granted his request.

A condemned man's dying wish, that's probably the way he saw it.

Let him see her, for all I care, he must have thought.

He has so little time left, he can't cause any trouble.

'I'll send her over this evening,' he said. 'After closing. Shall I have her bring you something?'

Homer shook his head.

'So you're really set on leaving for the other world, are you?'

Homer said nothing. He waited for McDonald to leave. Then he waited for sundown. About ten o'clock, he heard the typical noises of closing time. Clinking glasses, scraping chairs, long silences. Then the back door opened and there was a sound of approaching footsteps. Footsteps that were not McDonald's.

She might have been the female star of that great classic film footage of not-scientifically-attested events: *The Forbidden Planet*. She wore a little white dress just like the one Altaira wears in one of the opening sequences. And the very same stone necklace. She really did seem to be from another world. Altaira had been born on the forbidden planet, in a peaceful, magical garden, and had never met any man except her father. Homer wished the same were true of Molly, but McDonald had said she was from Las Vegas, and he'd heard there were plenty of men there.

But there was more. Altaira was beautiful, but her manner was somewhat old-fashioned. She was the classic sensible, devoted daughter, and this made her beauty somewhat insipid. Molly wasn't like that. She was more beautiful than Homer had dared to imagine – which was saying a lot, because when it came to imagination, he was pretty damn daring.

She had something about her of the girl next door, though if you knock at your neighbor's house, no girl like that will ever come to answer. It was impossible to take in all the details, such was her beauty. Her bone structure wasn't perfect and her figure wasn't anything special, but one look at her took your breath away.

Homer put this down to her complexion, which was as radiant as if she bathed her face in milk fifteen times a day. Perhaps it was only the effect of a special beauty cream, but her skin was white, so luminously white that at times it seemed positively ethereal. Everything around her looked dark in comparison. He would have worshiped her just for that. Homer adored the color white; it was a color that never failed to melt his heart, and it shouldn't be hard to guess why.

The distance between her eyebrows and her eyelids was slightly greater than average, just enough to make it seem as if her eyes were always closed. It was only one feature among many, but you couldn't help wondering about the reason for that expression; whether it was due to emotion or grief, to tiredness or a desire to tell you something; whether she was smiling or about to burst into tears.

She'd brought him an alienburger. At first he was reluctant to eat it, because he was afraid he'd throw up a few minutes later, which certainly wouldn't have made a good impression. He didn't want to put her off, let alone disgust her, though he had to admit it might be difficult not to. He *was* disgusting in his present state. Even he found himself disgusting. And he was a pretty easy-going guy.

'I thought you'd like it. Mac told me it was your favorite dish,' she said. She paused, then added: 'I made it specially for you.' Her words pierced him like a dagger.

He ate it.

When he had finished he couldn't think of anything to say. He looked around awkwardly and she did the same. They both sighed, each avoiding the other's eyes. When it seemed as if nothing else was going to happen, she brushed her hips lightly to straighten her dress, in a way that caught Homer's eye.

'Well, it's been nice meeting you,' she said. She was leaving, and there was nothing he could do to stop her. She was already standing in the doorway. Homer found the courage to speak her name. 'Molly?'

'Yeah?'

'Am I real bad?' Even he didn't know how he managed to get the words out.

She made one of those funny faces that people make at children. 'No, of course not.'

Homer said nothing. He hung his head, trying to take deep breaths because he was close to tears. One of those attacks of universal depression that he'd been subject to since he'd run out of heroin.

She must have noticed, because she sat down on the bed and said: 'Would you like to go for a walk outside? The air's cooler now and it'll do you good to stretch your legs. You're always cooped up in here.'

Homer didn't reply but it was obvious he wanted to go out into the night with her.

She helped him to his feet and out of the trailer. The air smelled of the lingering warmth of the day and tasted of desert dust. That taste reminded him of everything he'd lost in life, of the things that might have been.

'See? You can't be that bad if you can walk,' she said, looking at him in that way of hers.

That wasn't true. He was a fucking wreck, like he always was. But he needed to believe her. 'You think so?' he asked.

'Sure.'

His stomach pain was still there. He prayed he wouldn't bring up the hamburger. She said that 'sure' with a kind of enchanted sigh and there was a split-second of peace which almost banished the pain and made him forget he'd ever had a stomach. As soon as that moment had passed, the taste of the food he'd eaten came back up into his mouth, and the reality of the way he felt brutally snatched off the veil of foolish hope that he'd tried to lay over the corpse of his soul.

The night tastes of dust, in the desert.

She must think I'm pathetic, he thought. And he felt sad. If only he could have met Molly Resident in at least reasonable shape. Shape? The thought of the word made him wince. Nothing on earth could be more remote from the concept of shape than he was.

'There are a lot of trees where I come from.' He said this partly to give her an idea of how far away his home was and partly in an attempt to justify the state he was in. But also, he realized, because he was beginning to miss the trees.

He tried to conjure up an image of his present

shape. A wilting lettuce. Could such a beautiful girl ever be interested in a man like a wilting lettuce?

'I know.'

'You do?' said Homer, almost alarmed.

'Yeah. I know a lot about you,' and she looked at him with those big, fawnlike eyes. 'I know you've been hurt by a baseball and I know you went twenty years without sleeping. I have trouble sleeping too, sometimes. Or else I have such pointless dreams I wake up out of sheer boredom.'

'Did Mac tell you those things?'

'Mac and the lights people. You're a celebrity to them. They know all about you. Some of them know even more than I do.'

'Even more? Why should you know everything about me?'

'I'm your love from another world, don't you remember?' She shrugged and flashed him a smile that made him sick. Sick with desire.

'Oh yeah, that's right,' said Homer, disconsolately. She was so wonderfully herself, when she talked. So right. Everything that was wrong in him was missing from her.

'Can I ask you something?'

'Sure you can, Homer.'

'I was wondering. . .' He groped for the words. 'I was wondering if it bothered you, being my love from another world. Now you've met me, I mean.'

'It's just a job,' she replied, with childlike astonishment. 'It's not real.'

The hidden meaning of his question was as clear as that of her astonished reply. He was thinking about her in a particular way, that was the meaning of the question. And the meaning of the reply was that he mustn't think of her that way. But Homer couldn't help himself. He felt he'd die if he were forced to stop.

'It's not real, but everyone thinks you're my love from another world. Everyone except me. Isn't that strange?' He was hoping to get her to say something that would authorize him to continue thinking as he did, but she said she was beginning to feel tired, it had been nice meeting him but maybe it was time to turn in now.

That night Homer didn't sleep a wink. Just like in the old days.

Contrary to McDonald's expectations, Homer did not die. In fact, in some ways he actually seemed to get better. He was the same fuck-up as before, the fuck-up he'd been ever since the emptying of the baseball. But now he was a fuck-up with motivation. A fuck-up that had found a vague desire to live and was trying to summon up what little strength it had left. But in his attempts to pick himself up he was even more pathetic than before, if that was possible. There was no doubt that McDonald would rather see him dead, but it was equally clear that he wasn't going to die as soon as McDonald seemed to be hoping. Not with Molly Resident in the neighborhood, at any rate. She was his motivation, she kept him alive.

McDonald was going out of his mind. He hated the feeling that his hands were tied, that he couldn't do anything to change the situation. He couldn't send Molly away, because that would leave him without any attraction for Home Base. But if he didn't send her away, Homer wouldn't die. Which was even worse, in a way. A normal Homer was unpredictable enough. God help him with a love-sick Homer around the place.

To limit the damage, he decided to make a deal. He told Homer he would let him receive the occasional visit from Molly, but in return he must promise never to set foot in Home Base again. 'I've told them you've gone to the forbidden planet to ask Molly's father for her hand in marriage. You mustn't let anyone see you around, it'd ruin everything. You do understand that, don't you?'

'Gone to the forbidden planet to ask for her hand in marriage? What kind of crap is that?'

'I had to tell them something.'

'You might have told them something less dumb.'

'The lights people were over the moon when they heard about it. The weirder the stories, the more they like them.'

'Okay, but if that's the case, one day I get to come back with her father's approval and marry Molly,' said Homer defiantly.

'Oh, I don't doubt that for a moment. But it doesn't make much difference.'

'Of course it does.'

'From your point of view, maybe. But nothing will change around here.'

Homer didn't follow.

'You see, Homer, I've put it around that the forbidden planet is seven light years away from Earth and that by the time you get back we'll all be long dead. But Molly's from another world. Maybe she'll still be alive and you'll be able to marry her,' said McDonald, with a loud guffaw, barely suppressing his delight at his brilliant scheme.

Homer was speechless. He's planning to kill me, he thought. Why don't you say out loud that you're planning to kill me? So his suspicions had been right. He hadn't been imagining things. That lardass burger-maker was going to kill him, and all for the sake of a broken-down shack in the middle of the desert that he had the nerve to call a bar.

McDonald sat down on the bed and patted Homer's right thigh. He's after something, thought Homer.

'You like her, don't you?' said McDonald with a knowing look.

Homer waited to see what he was driving at.

'Well, let me tell you something.' McDonald left a calculated pause. 'She's not your kind of girl. I know she's attractive. And I know she may seem to be kinda affectionate. But she doesn't give a shit about you. You're not her type and you never will be. You can't seriously think a fox like that would go for a loser like you. You haven't got a prayer, you'll just make her hate you.'

'. . .'

'You'll never make her love you.'

'. . .'

'I know, you think the fact that she comes to see you and brings you your food and talks to you must mean something.'

That was exactly what he thought.

'Well, it doesn't mean a fucking thing.'

'...'

'She does it because that's the way women are. Some women, anyway. She's just a professional, doing her job. She's kind to you because she's paid to be.'

'...'

'I bet she hasn't told you what she did in Las Vegas.'

'...'

'Oh no, she hasn't. You've got no idea. Well, I'll tell you. She worked in a lapdancing club. Writhing around a metal bar, half-naked. Have you ever been in one of those places, Homer?'

'...'

'No you haven't. Any fool can see that. You don't know a fucking thing. You think she's so sweet and vulnerable. A poor little girl trying to scrape a living in the hope that one day she'll meet someone who understands her.'

'...'

'Bullshit.'

'...'

'Listen, I know you're going through a hard time. The desert, the baseball thing. It's easy to lose your grip when you're down. But you just watch out. Look,

I'd tell you to fuck her and have done with it if there was a snowball's chance in hell of her letting you fuck her. But there isn't. Don't delude yourself.'

'. . .'

'D'you understand me, boy?'

'. . .'

'Never.'

'. . .'

'. . .'

'Why not?'

'For fuck's sake, boy. You're even stupider than I thought.'

He didn't believe a word of what McDonald told him, but as far as Molly was concerned he feared he was right: he didn't have a prayer. He must be realistic: he looked like he'd just crawled out of a dump. He'd fucked up right down the line: he'd run out of money, maybe he didn't even have his house in Aberdeen anymore. He was paranoid that it had been confiscated because he hadn't paid his taxes lately. In fact, he wasn't sure if he'd ever paid them.

And he'd emptied his baseball; there was another problem. If he could have systemized himself with just a tiny bit of heroin, maybe he could have thought of something interesting to say to her; maybe he could have looked more presentable and, who knows, maybe he could even have impressed her. Who could rule it out? You never knew what you could do with the right dose of heroin.

Heroine.

Had she been a powdered system and not a woman, it would all have been so easy. He wouldn't have had to worry about how disgusting he was, the money he no longer had and the interesting things he couldn't find to say to her. She would have loved him. Unconditionally. Blind love in the true sense of the word, no shit. All you have to do is want her and there she is. Always available.

'. . .'

Well, maybe not always.

'. . .'

Fuck, how sick he felt.

'. . .'

But shit, he did like Molly. Maybe he liked her even more than heroin, but he didn't dare investigate that heresy.

I am heroine, your love.

Thou shalt have no other heroine before me.

Thou shalt not take the name of heroine in vain.

All men are equal before heroine.

You have the right to make one phone call.

You have the right to a lawyer.

You have the right to remain silent.

Anything you say may be used against you.

'. . .'

I love you.

Events were coming to a head – even Homer realized that. Like McDonald, he felt his hands were tied, though for different reasons. Had he been a rational person he'd have left Rachel, he'd have gotten out of that godforsaken place as soon as possible. It didn't matter that he was broke; McDonald would have been only too glad to give him all the money he needed, just so long as he went. But that would mean giving up Molly, which was something he just couldn't face.

Although the story was just an invention of McDonald's, Molly was the only love he'd found on his long journey from the forests of the Northwest. Maybe she wasn't from another world, but she was so goddamn pretty. And so goddamn vulnerable. Such at least was the idea he had formed of her, and he wasn't about to change it. He couldn't leave such a helpless young maid – fuck it, how he liked that word! – in the hands of a cynical profiteer like McDonald. He would have thought up some plan to run away with her, but he doubted if Molly would ever give up her starring role as the love from another world to run off with a reject from this one. Deep down in his soul he knew McDonald was right: she would never let him love her. But since he'd sniffed away his soul along with all the heroin he'd used over the years, he didn't give a damn whether McDonald was right or not. Fuck McDonald and his rightness, that was Homer's take on the matter. Besides, everybody knows that true love doesn't care about right or wrong. What kind of love would it be if it did?

So, although the odds were stacked against him, he flatly refused to stop thinking about her. He was determined to play out all his cards to the end, though now and then a mean little voice would whisper in his brain, What cards?

Never mind what cards, he snapped. Anyway, I'm not leaving. If I can't take her away with me, I'm going to stay here in Rachel with her, said Homer.

Suit yourself, said the voice.

But he couldn't just not go away. He must do something, he must be bold. He'd never performed a single bold action in his life. His heroic deeds, such as staying awake for twenty years, were the instinctive reflexes of a turtle. He'd withdrawn into sleeplessness in self-defense, because he was afraid they would get him if he slept, and he'd only started sleeping again when he'd discovered a protective system, a shell made of heroin. But now he'd reached the point where he had nothing to lose. He'd run out of heroin and money, he'd lost his house, he didn't know where Kurt was. Who could help him out here, beyond the bounds of the desert? All he was left with was the weakness of despair. And Molly, of course.

So, despite his weakness and the unlikelihood of his ever impressing Molly, he made up his mind to stop acting like a turtle and do something real, something shell-like.

But he was forgetting one thing. It's strange that he'd forgotten it, because it was something Kurt never tired of repeating – that turtles' shells aren't the protective covering everyone thinks they are. If you knock on the shell it hurts them. And if they fall on their back, it splits open and they die.

*　　*　　*

This is what happened.

One evening Molly asked Homer about his trips into the hills. 'I hear you've found a lot of things up there,' she said. 'Even an old photograph of a young Indian couple.'

Homer nodded.

'Mac told me you burned it.' The way she said this, it was like she and Homer had been the young couple in the photograph. Homer read a whole world of meanings into those words, the world as he would have liked it to be.

'I'd never burn a photograph of you,' muttered Homer. What a dumb thing to say. He realized that even as he was saying it.

She shrugged and said: 'Well, it was only a photo.' She frowned for a moment and added: 'You know what? I'm going to burn all my photographs before I get old. I don't want to be reminded how pretty I was when I was young, and feel sad.'

'A beautiful woman remains beautiful all her life.' This was even dumber than his first remark. Where the hell had he got it from? He wasn't the kind of guy to talk such sentimental crap. Yet he'd said it.

'Don't be stupid,' said Molly.

Homer looked crestfallen.

'What are you moping about?' she asked, pretending not to understand.

Homer couldn't bring himself to say anything.

Molly gave him a little shove on the arm.

'Hey.'

Finally he managed to say, 'I'm sorry.'

'What for?'

'For saying something so stupid.'

'Oh, come on. If you only knew how many stupid things I say.'

Homer was about to say that that couldn't be true, but luckily had the presence of mind to restrain himself.

Molly's face suddenly lit up. Homer always melted away when he saw that expression. 'Why don't you take me to the abandoned mines?' She sounded like a little girl, and that gave Homer confidence, deluding him that he could keep the situation under control.

'Well, we could go to Logan's mine, but it's quite a long way.'

'It can't be further than Las Vegas.'

'It's about thirty miles.'

Molly looked at him, wide-eyed with amazement.

'Wow.'

'Yeah.'

'And you used to walk there?'

'Yeah.'

'That's a hell of a long way. It must take ages to get there.'

'Seven hours there and seven hours back,' he said. 'Roughly.'

'You must have been pretty fit in those days.'

'I had my baseball.'

336   Molly smiled, awkwardly. 'Well, since you don't have it anymore, we could go in the pickup,' she suggested, with a shrug. Homer noticed that she often did that. It was another thing about her that made him melt away. Those things were becoming too numerous to count.

'I don't have a pickup.'

'I know. But we could take Mac's.'

'He'd never give it to me.'

'Not even if I asked him?'

'Huh?' It was a long time since he'd last said huh.

'I think he'll give it to me.'

Homer thought so too, and they were both proved right. Molly was astute enough not to tell McDonald the real reason why she wanted it. She told him she had to go to Las Vegas to see an old friend. McDonald gave her a day off and the keys to the pickup. He wasn't too happy about it, he could tell she was lying, but he had no choice. He just couldn't say no to that girl.

Homer could hardly believe it was happening. He and she together in McDonald's pickup, heading for the abandoned mines. A whole day to spend with the only woman he'd ever loved, in fact probably the only one he'd ever talked to for more than ten consecutive minutes.

The two of them alone in the desert, in a wilderness that shielded them from any interference. Not a living soul, only an animal's skull gleaming white in the distance. Or maybe it was just the reflection of a white rock.

White, like Molly's skin. It was the first time he'd seen her in daylight and the brightness of her face almost hurt his eyes, such was its intensity. She was dressed like the girl from the forbidden planet, as on the evening they'd first met. Her arms, bare and taut on the wheel, were whiter than her dress. She must use some kind of fluorescent cream to make her skin shine like that, Homer thought to himself.

'Your skin's so white.'

Molly smiled, without taking her eyes off the road.

'Is that its real color?'

'What color should it be?'

'I don't know. Skin color.'

Molly smiled again. 'I'll tell you a secret.'

'There's a secret?'

'Beer.'

'Huh?'

'A famous actress used to put it on her hair. She said it made it shine on camera. I decided to try it on my skin. I figured that if it didn't work, I could always drink it.'

Homer eyed her furtively. He couldn't work out if she was telling the truth or just joking.

She added: 'When I'm old enough, of course.'

'Old enough?'

'To drink, honey. I've heard that in some states girls aren't allowed to drink alcohol until they come of age. Maybe it applies to boys too, I don't know.'

Homer thought this over. 'You mean you're under twenty-one?'

Molly turned toward him. 'You really believe everything you're told, don't you?'

'No, it's just that I don't like it when people don't tell me the truth.'

'The truth.' Her eyes were on the road again now. 'A rattlesnake that doesn't bite teaches you nothing, my mom used to say.'

'It was Jessamyn West who said that, not your mom.'

'What are you talking about?'

'I read it in a dictionary of quotations in the Aberdeen Public Library.'

'Well, my mom said it too. They must have read the same quotation.'

'Who?'

'My mother and that West woman, you fool.'

'Jessamyn West didn't need to read it, it was her who said it.'

'You know you can be really boring sometimes? What are you trying to prove, that I didn't tell you the truth? Well, what if I didn't?'

Homer stared at her. She stretched out her hand and stroked his cheek with the back of it. 'You mustn't frown like that when things don't go the way you want them to. It's just the way life is – one day every-thing's fine, next day you meet a girl who tells you lies. There's nothing you can do about it.'

'Why?'

'Why should I tell you lies, you mean? I told you, a rattlesnake that doesn't bite teaches you nothing.'

Homer felt confused. He looked out of the window. The silhouette of Mount Irish had begun to ruffle the flat line of the horizon. 'You haven't answered me.'

'Did you ask me a question?'

'Are you under twenty-one?'

'Who knows? Maybe I am, maybe I'm not. I've told you the truth this time, are you happy now?'

'You've told me nothing.'

'So what?'

'I don't understand why you do it.'

'You don't understand women. That's different.'

Molly's expression suddenly clouded over, as if her mind was elsewhere. Homer wondered what she was thinking about, because she certainly wasn't thinking about him.

They were silent for a while – she driving, her mind on some distant planet that Homer would never reach, he watching the dusty rocks rush by, his mind on a sequence from that film footage of the invasion of the body snatchers. Or rather, on a kind of apocryphal sequence that he was imagining now. Homer and Molly were the stars, playing Dr Miles Bennell and Becky Driscoll. It's near the end of the story, when Miles and Becky are hiding in the doctor's office. Night has fallen, and the people of Santa Mira, now all taken over by the body snatchers, are hunting for them, to catch them and make them sleep. Perhaps there are two of those big pods lying ready for them outside the door. Miles thinks back to the evening when Becky had come to his studio to talk to him about Wilma's uncle who was no longer Wilma's uncle. Becky had worn a long-sleeved white silk blouse that evening. The same blouse she's wearing now. He remembers how happy he'd been to see her again after so long, and realizes he's never forgotten her in all these years, although there was nothing between them in the past, except a couple of dates in their high-school days. Only now does he understand. Only now does he know what he wants. Well, since you know, be bold. Do something, thought Homer. So he made Dr Miles say: 'I love you, Becky.' Just at that moment, Miles hears a sound behind the door. A kind of faint rustling noise. So faint that perhaps he only imagined it, because Becky doesn't seem to have noticed anything. So Homer made Dr Miles add: 'I wish we were married, Becky. I wish we were husband and wife.' Becky looks at him with those cartoon-fawn eyes that are so similar to Molly's. So Homer made Becky say something too: 'I wish that too. Why didn't we get married?' But it's too late for wondering why, so Homer made Dr Miles keep silent, preferring to let Becky speak again. 'We should have done, but you were afraid. Afraid of me, afraid we'd be happy.' Dr Miles knows she's right, he *was* afraid, but since all seems lost, with the body snatchers hot on their trail, he also knows that there's no point in being afraid now. The time for reasons and fears is past. So Homer made Dr Miles say: 'Maybe there's still time.' Of course there is, thought Homer. There's still time for you, just as there's still time for me with Molly. Maybe McDonald's right, maybe I'm not the man for her and she'll never love me. But why should I worry about the words of someone whose only wish is for me to disappear? It's Molly I should be thinking about. And me, thought Homer. He sensed it would never work between them. If the morning's weather foretells the day, as the proverb says, their bickering over such a trivial matter as the Jessamyn West quotation didn't augur well. What difference did it make now? He had nothing to lose, so he might as well ruin everything. But with her in his arms, with his fingers in her hair and his lips on hers. He wanted those cartoon-fawn eyes and that white skin and he didn't care whether it was the beer that caused it, or what. So he decided to turn toward her to say the same things he had made Dr Miles say, but just as he was about to do it, when it seemed to him as if he had already done it, the rustle he'd heard in the apocryphal scene became a noise so loud it stabbed him hard in the stomach. So he turned in the opposite direction, shouted to Molly to stop, opened the door and threw himself on the ground, groveling in the dust, coughing and vomiting up everything that he thought he no longer had inside him, till he awoke, lying exhausted on the ground with Molly on her knees beside him, gazing at him in concern.

They weren't in the desert anymore, but indoors, in a dark place where there wasn't enough air. Or maybe it was just that night had fallen.

'Where are we?' he asked.

'In the abandoned mine.'

So they were. Night hadn't fallen. Now he was beginning to distinguish the details and recognize his surroundings. The tunnel hewn out of the rock, the shoring of now-rotten beams, the shaft that vanished into a dark hole. Logan's abandoned mine, which he had so often explored. There was even a little pool of water, like in the mine where Becky and Miles sheltered in the real finale of the invasion of the body snatchers.

Molly urged him to get up and rinse his face in the pool. 'Can you do it?' she asked him.

'Of course I can,' he replied indignantly.

He staggered over to the pool, with Molly still supporting him. Contact with the water made him feel better but his stomach was burning as if it had been scoured with a cloth soaked in hydrochloric acid.

'Mac's right,' sighed Molly.

'What d'you mean?' Homer said agitatedly.

'You're not well. That's twice you've vomited and passed out today.'

'Twice?'

'Yeah, first in the pickup, now here in the mine.'

Homer's mind was a blank. The last thing he remembered was the apocryphal scene of the invasion of the body snatchers where Miles declares himself to Becky. Mac's right, he repeated to himself. That's what she said, Mac's right. Her words were proof that McDonald wanted to get rid of him. First he'd used him to promote his seedy little joint, now he wanted to eliminate him in case he spoiled things. He'd found a new attraction so alluring it would make everyone forget the old one and arouse entirely new appetites in those dickhead tourists. McDonald must have advised her not to waste too much time on Homer, because, thank God, he wasn't going to be around much longer. He'd probably even suggested she put him out of his misery.

You devious fucking bastard, Homer thought. Not only do you want me dead, you want her to kill me for you.

He looked Molly in the eyes. She replied with a smile that Homer found impossible to interpret. Molly was right, too: he didn't understand women. He couldn't decipher the signs they used instead of words, that way they had of always meaning something different from what they said. Molly belonged to him. He'd been asked the question, What about love? And he deserved the answer, especially after traveling mile upon mile to find her, and losing the only things in the world that loved him: Kurt, heroine, the trees in the woods around Aberdeen. No, he said to himself. It was his question, and it was his answer. And he wasn't going to let some two-bit burger-maker take them away from him.

If there was any justice in the world, Molly should be his. The most elementary principle of natural law demanded that she should be. But with his inability to understand women and to decipher Molly's smile, he couldn't be sure that McDonald hadn't talked her round, that the scheming son of a bitch hadn't won her over and she was no longer his love from another world, the girl with skin that shone like a glass of milk lit from within and with eyes like those of a cartoon fawn.

Even if there had been something in that smile, some hint that Molly was only one of the countless different people who wander around the world, Homer would probably never have spotted it, or if by chance he had, he wouldn't have been able to decipher it.

No, he didn't understand women. But he was tired. He felt the fatigue of all the years he'd spent without sleeping and of those he'd spent wishing he didn't have a stomach. He felt every single one of those years, and he no longer had the strength. He was tired. He was just too tired, and he might as well know. So he said the words he'd made Miles say.

'I love you, Molly.'

She frowned. 'What? Are you kidding?'

'No, I really do love you.'

'But we hardly know each other. You don't know anything about me.'

'I wish we were married, Molly.'

She sprang to her feet. 'You're sick. We'd better get back to Rachel.' She made as if to turn toward the entrance of the mine but Homer threw himself to the side and grabbed one of her legs with both hands, bringing her down. She kicked out, then took off a shoe and hit Homer on the head, but he clung to her leg.

'Let me go,' she screamed.

Pinning her leg down with the weight of his body, Homer managed to grab her wrist. He prized the shoe out of her hand and threw it into the pool. Then he dug his fingers into her arms and started to climb up her body, crawling over it. She kept sobbing to him to leave her alone and she must be truly sweet and vulnerable if a man at the end of his strength could pin her down so easily. Now his face was level with her breast. He smelled the scent of her body emanate from her dress and he laid his ear on her to listen to the beating of her heart. Then he sniffed her neck, brushed her ear with his lips, licked her hair. Finally he pulled himself up just far enough to be able to look into her eyes and, still keeping her pinned to the ground, said: 'I really do love you. I'm not afraid of you, believe me.'

She was trembling all over, shaking her head, her eyes full of tears. Her mouth was open but she wasn't speaking. She seemed unable to breathe. He looked at her for a moment longer then plunged his face into the girl's open mouth and kissed it and tasted her saliva while he dug his fingers further and further into her arms, gripped her so tight he felt the hardness of her bones. She whimpered in desperation, then suddenly seemed to give in. She stopped resisting, but she hadn't really surrendered. She was only in a kind of faint. She lay as still as a corpse. Homer thought of the dead body of Laura Palmer. He slackened his grip on her arms, withdrew his lips from her mouth and looked at her. She wasn't dead, only stiff. Her expression was no longer that cartoon-fawn gaze, but a glare of hatred. He'd reached the point McDonald had foretold. He'd made her hate him.

'I really do love you,' he stammered.

She continued to stare at him, coldly. She no longer seemed so sweet and vulnerable. She could have brushed Homer's body off her with a wave of her hand. Even her skin wasn't so white anymore.

'I'm not what you think I am,' she said to him at length. 'And you're just a poor, sick, unhappy little boy.'

All of a sudden Molly's face was transformed before his eyes. He saw the close-up of Becky's face, her blank expression in the closing sequence, when Miles, after kissing her, realizes that she has slept, that she too is now a body snatcher.

Like Dr Miles, Homer retreated from Molly, took a few steps backward, shaking his head, turned and fled, terror-stricken, toward the entrance of the mine.

'Where are you going?' he heard Molly say behind him. 'You can't hide, Boddah!'

But Homer didn't stop. He kept on running. He

reached State Highway 375 and didn't stop running. He ran for all he was worth, till the town of Rachel was just a cluster of white dots behind him; he ran till even those white dots were no longer visible; he ran till he was alone in the middle of nowhere.

He ran.

7.

Alter Echo

Lovers of raw facts may like to know that, after his flight from Rachel, nothing more was heard of Homer Alienson for a long time. Nothing more was heard until early April 1994, when there were several sightings of him in Seattle.

He was seen wandering around in his usual uniform: the red bandanna, the logger's shirt, the worn, faded jeans, the Converse Chuck Taylors. He was seen near the home of Jimi Hendrix. He was seen in a gunstore buying a twenty-gauge shotgun, a weapon recommended for personal defense in the home because the bullets don't penetrate walls and there's no danger of hitting another member of your family in the next room. He was seen in the Blue Moon Tavern, where the famous bum Jack Kerouac once stopped by for a drink. He sat at a table – Homer, not Kerouac – gazing down for hours at a glass, which was probably empty, clutching it tightly with both hands. Some kids stared in at him from the street, the palms of their hands flattened against the window, but he didn't notice. Perhaps they'd mistaken him for Kurt, who by now was a famous rock star. He was seen taking a taxi to 171 Lake Washington Boulevard, the address of the house that Kurt and his wife Love had bought. Some, however, believe that it wasn't Homer at all, but Kurt, who had also disappeared during that very same period. It was certainly very easy to confuse them. By that stage they were practically indistinguishable, and even if it had been possible to tell the difference, what could it possibly have mattered by then whether the person who was seen on any particular occasion was Homer rather than Kurt or, which seems more likely, that it was sometimes one and sometimes the other?

It was an employee of Veca Electrical Contractors of Bellevue who found the body. It was the morning of April 8th, a Friday. The electrician had been sent there to install a security system. Having entered through the front door, he went into the backyard to see if there was a way of bringing the wire around.

He saw the body through the French doors. At first he thought it was a mannequin, but then he saw that there was blood by the ear. Finally he saw the shotgun resting on the mannequin's chest, and more blood. The barrel was pointing at the mouth. Mannequins don't shoot themselves in the mouth, he thought. He rushed out to his van and radioed his head office to call 911, because there was a body.

At 10.45 the detectives arrive on the scene. The electrician says he came to do some work on the electrical wiring and saw the victim lying on the floor in the greenhouse above the garage. Fire units force entry by breaking a pane in the French doors and confirm that the victim is dead.

The victim is lying on his back with his head facing east and his feet west. His skull shattered by a gunshot. There is a large pool of coagulated blood. There is a twenty-gauge Remington shotgun pointing at the victim's head. In the pocket of one of the victim's garments the receipt of purchase is found. Serial number 1088925. Price, three hundred and eight dollars, thirty-seven cents. Date, March 30th, 1994. There are several cigarette butts scattered on the floor. There is a can of Barq's root beer, also on the floor. There are one hundred twenty dollars in cash, also on the floor, to the right of the victim. There is a cigar box. There are syringes, burnt spoons, cotton and pieces of a tar-like substance; these things are all in the cigar box. On the walls there are some stainless steel planting trays. On one of these trays there is a little pile of dirt with bulbs in it. On top of the pile there is a letter written in red ink. It is addressed to a certain Boddah.

After eleven o'clock, the forensic pathologist examines the body and declares that the damage to the oral cavity indicates that the shot was taken in the mouth. He inspects the victim's forearms and finds puncture marks. The autopsy reveals traces of Valium in the body and a quantity of heroin that would be considerable even for an addict with a high tolerance to the drug.

A few days later the police closed the case, stating that the victim had killed himself by a self-inflicted gunshot wound to the head. His body was identified as that of Kurt, but today we know that Homer B. Alienson, too, after reading Kurt's letter to him, put that same shotgun in his mouth and pulled the trigger. Apparently no one heard the shot, but the sound echoed in the vast, rainy world of the dull Northwest to which Homer had returned, in the depths of those dense woods where the sun never shines.

When the shot was fired the television was on.

One last thing.

    You might think Homer Alienson killed himself because of Molly Resident. That is not so. He killed himself because of Kurt, because he was Boddah.

    You might think Kurt killed himself because of his wife. That is not so. On the day of his funeral his wife said: 'That's all bullshit. But I'll tell you something: that Eighties tough love thing is bullshit too. I should have let him – we all should have let him – have his numbness. We should have let him have it, instead of trying to strip away his skin.' Perhaps she was referring to those flowers whose scent is so powerful that anyone who breathes it falls asleep. Perhaps she meant that if we hadn't tried to strip the scent of those flowers away from Kurt, he would have gone on sleeping forever, instead of dying.

    One thing's for sure. Kurt and Boddah loved one another. They were true friends. Bosom buddies. Kurt fought like hell to prove that Boddah existed. His aunt still preserves one piece of evidence of those battles Kurt had fought ever since he was a little boy.

It's a recording. Kurt used to love playing with tape recorders when he was small, and his aunt had one with a reverb unit. Kurt would say 'Boddah' into the microphone. The reverb would answer: 'Boddah.' Kurt would laugh happily: 'He did it.' He'd put the microphone to his mouth again and say: 'Boddah.' The reverb would answer, and Kurt would laugh: 'He did it, he did it again.' He'd repeat the experiment over and over. He'd repeat it to the point of exhaustion, as children do, in their sweet assurance that eternity concerns them.

The reverb never let Kurt down, it always answered him. He'd repeat: 'He did it, he did it,' and laugh happily. He'd laugh as children do, with squeals of mysterious power and inexplicable bliss.

Those squeals, too, can be heard in Kurt's aunt's recording. It's a sound like the one some rubber dolls make when you squeeze them in your hand.

Author's Note

Many of the events recounted in this novel either belong wholly to the realm of fiction or have been so radically altered that they bear no relation to biographical truth, if such a thing exists. Nevertheless the reader will notice that many other events, and many personal and place names, are more or less explicitly related to the real world. In short, this is a classic case of a work which is a blend of fact and fiction, the product of an attitude which some may despise but which is as old as human civilization itself.

To attempt to explain which side of the balance hangs lower in this case strikes me as a pointless exercise, but even if I wanted to I wouldn't be capable of it. The writing of a novel entails a heightened state of imaginative empathy where it is easy to lose oneself and where the border between the shared reality of the world and everything else is blurred and elusive. That is my opinion, at any rate.

When I started work on *Love-Shaped Story* I had no intention of writing about Kurt Cobain. My idea was simply to tell a love story about a bizarre individual who has convinced himself that he doesn't exist, travels the roads of America and falls in love with a stripper whom he mistakes for a beautiful alien from a forbidden planet. I decided to set part of the action in Aberdeen, Washington State, in the early Nineties, because I needed a gloomy, desolate scenario. Only later did I start to think about Kurt Cobain. Aberdeen is a very small town, and it seemed to me unlikely that my character would not have met the leader of Nirvana at least once. They might even have been friends. In general I am inclined to be mistrustful of what is probable, but in this case the idea of such a meeting was a temptation I just couldn't resist. So I decided to raise the stakes still further by making my character Kurt's imaginary friend.

They say reality often reawakens the imagination. Whether that is true or not I don't know. What I do know is that for over two years I immersed myself in the tragic life of an unusually sensitive young man who killed himself at age twenty-seven. I read as much about him as I could and listened to his wonderful songs so often that Kurt Cobain became the best friend that I had never had but so much needed. I am aware that hundreds of thousands of other people feel the same way about him, but I'm not claiming to be original. Even today, whenever I think about him too intensely, tears come to my eyes. If the same thing happens to others, that's no problem. On the contrary, it means they'll understand what I'm talking about.

There is another thing of which I am sure. If ever my imagination has been reawakened by reality, I owe it to the writers who have told the story of Kurt Cobain before me. The bibliography is, of course, vast, but I owe a particular debt to Charles R. Cross, who in his *Heavier than Heaven: The Biography of Kurt Cobain* showed rare humanity in his handling of a controversial and delicate subject. Anyone who wants to know what the leader of Nirvana was really like should read this excellent book.

Just as important to me was the equally fine *Come As You Are: The Story of Nirvana* by Michael Azerrad, who was fortunate enough to know Cobain at first hand.

I would also like to mention *Nevermind: Nirvana,* by Jim Berkenstadt and Charles R. Cross, which provides a wealth of detail on the recording of the album *Nevermind* and helped with the background of chapter five.

Fiction, too, must have its acknowledgements. My viewing of the TV serials created by Gene Rodenberry and David Lynch, *Star Trek* and *Twin Peaks*, and of Don Siegel's film *Invasion of the Body Snatchers*, played a vital part in the conception of my novel. I also found it useful to dip into *The Star Trek Compendium*, by Allan Asherman, and *Full Of Secrets: Critical Approaches to 'Twin Peaks'*, edited by David Lavery.

The town of Rachel, Nevada, which I describe in the sixth chapter, is simply a surreal caricature of a real place where things can be seen which almost certainly do not exist. The amazing truth about this place is told in Phil Patton's excellent reportage, *Dreamland: Travels Inside The Secret World Of Roswell and Area 51*. I mention this book simply because it is very good, and good books are always important in one way or another.

Should anyone who had the privilege of actually knowing Kurt Cobain object that *their* Kurt – the man they knew and loved – was nothing like *my* Kurt, they would be right. Not for a single moment did I search for the truth. I wouldn't have known what to do with it if I had found it, and in any case it doesn't belong to me. Sometimes I like to imagine that Cobain might have quite liked my version of Boddah, but my heightened state of imaginative empathy does not blind me to the fact that that is a meaningless thing to say. All I can do is to repeat that what the real Kurt did was simply to reawaken my imagination. If I am honest, he also reawakened my pain. But that is of no importance.